Revolvo and Other Canadian Tales

Revolvo and Other Canadian Tales

by

Steve Lundin

TSAR
Toronto
1997

We acknowledge the support of the Canada Council for the Arts for our publishing program. We also acknowledge support from the Ontario Arts Council.

Cover art: *Breaking Prairie in July, NWT, Canada* by Edward Roper, National Archives of Canada.

Canadian Cataloguing in Publication Data

Lundin, Steve
    Revolvo and other Canadian tales

ISBN 0-920661-58-0

I. Title.

PS8573.U543R48 1997   C813'.54   C97-932228-6
PR9199.3.L86R48 1997

Printed in Canada by Coach House Printing.

TSAR Publications
P. O. Box 6996, Station A
Toronto, Ontario M5W 1X7
Canada

This book is dedicated to
Bowen Thomas-Lundin,
the new kid on the Factory floor

Acknowledgements

I would like to express my gratitude to my friends and family whose support has helped make this book possible. Special mention is accorded Susan Thomas and Peter Knowlson, for their hospitality; Chris and Val at the Bosh Pub, and the staff at the Spotted Dog, for their kindness (and the generous supply of juice for my laptop); Martin Callaghan for the voice in the wilderness; those in the Common; and Clare for her love and patience.

Contents

Machines

WILL OFFSTEAD'S prosthetic left hand held the wheel unerringly as he worked through the gears. The intricate machinery that began at his elbow was encased in flesh-coloured plastic, shiny as if sheathed in sweat.

Through the tinted windshield the highway reached out ahead of him in a straight line, black topped and barren. In the yellow blur of the countryside patches of snow appeared like unpainted spots on a canvas, textured and almost translucent in the sharp cold sunlight. Stands of alder cloaked the low hills with a mantle of dull grey, derelict barns the hue of dried blood appearing every now and then alongside them.

Leaning forward as if nailed to the wheel, Will pushed the Kenworth up to cruising speed, his grey eyes fixed on the black highway as it poured like liquid into the grilled maw of his hungry machine.

Jaws working on a wad of Beeman's, Will ran his hand through his thick black hair in a jerking motion, raking his nails against his scalp until it tingled. The west horizon was a grey mass of clouds building in front of him, piling higher and higher and swelling obesely at the sides. Snow for sure, he muttered to himself. No need to check the radio. No need to check anything.

He flicked his eyes to the three mirrors in quick succession, then turned them back to the road. Nothing back there, nothing at all. His whole body ached as if every muscle and every ligament had been stretched beyond their limit then locked there. His bones felt brittle as wire. But there was nothing back there, not a goddamn thing.

The inside of the cab stank of burnt rubber—he could smell it in the cloth, the plastic, the metal; and air fresheners didn't work a damn. Reaching into his breast pocket he pulled out another stick of gum, unwrapped it one-handed and jammed it into his mouth.

There was a truckstop up ahead, ten miles this side of Billings. No one

1

ever used it anymore, since the interstate had been widened and resurfaced. No one used this highway at all, it seemed. Will preferred the milk routes; they were more peaceful, less trafficked. He could clamp his claws on the wheel and roll on forever without a thing getting in his way.

The road took on a grade and the Kenworth began to growl the music of a metal animal. Gearing down, Will leaned forward, his ribs feeling like they were about to split open under the strain. The loads were getting heavier each time out. Machine parts, tons of them—the whole country seemed to be held together by machine parts, bolts rattling, metal straining; the whole country wheezed and whirred and parts were breaking down everywhere. Will could feel the load on his back, a crushing weight dragging him back down the grade. He was nearing the top of the rise, engine roaring, the cab shaking with effort. Then he reached it, and a valley sprawled out before him, the small dingy Gas Cafe squatting on its floor like a forgotten toy.

The stormclouds had swallowed the sun and the afternoon had grown dim and dull edged. Clutch out, Will brought the semi down into the valley slowly, the weight of his load seeming to push him, striving to grind him down into the ground. His foot was leaden as he eased down on the airbrakes. The Kenworth hissed and he swung it into the turn-off and stopped beyond the lone gas pump. With a sigh he unclamped his grip on the wheel and shut her down.

He rubbed fog off the window and looked over at the cafe. Lights were on inside it, but there was otherwise no sign of life. Will opened the door and climbed down onto the cracked and buckled asphalt. The wind was bitterly cold, blowing in from the north, crossing the front of the storm. He walked over to the entrance, his eyes searching through the cluttered window. He couldn't see anyone but found the door unlocked. Warm air swept around him as he stepped inside and closed the door behind him.

The tables were set but unoccupied. An overhead heater churned out hot air with a rattle. "Hello? Anybody here?"

A sound came from the kitchen and a young woman stepped out and stood behind the counter. Her gaze flicked over Will's shoulder to the white Kenworth sitting outside, then turned back to his face.

She was short, mousy haired and plump. Her round face was youthful and complex, bearing the last traces of adolescence with weary impatience. "This place open?" Will asked.

She frowned, shifted from one foot to the other, then replied in a wavering voice, "Not really. Season's over and we've closed up." She placed a hand on one hip. "Sam's not around—he owns the place. I'm just cleaning up. I don't think the pump's working."

Will shook his head. "Don't need gas. Just a cup of coffee and maybe a slice of pie."

The woman bit her lip, then shrugged. "Okay."

Will took off his coat and sat down at a table. Looking out of the window he saw a row of wrecks: rusting, seized-up tractors and combines; twisted and crushed cars, pickups and trucks squatting in the frozen frost-sprinkled mud. His gaze stopped on the wreck of a VW Bug. It was hardly recognizable: corkscrew torqued with shreds of metal sticking out everywhere. Christ, Will muttered silently. After a moment he turned his head around and watched the woman spooning coffee into a filter.

The cafe was small; stools and chairs were covered in red vinyl, the tabletops in red formica with gold and silver flecks. A jukebox stood in one corner, dark and silent. The air smelled musty and dry, unused.

"Coffee'll be ready in a minute," the woman said, turning with a smile that froze as she saw his arm where it rested on the tabletop, the two steel fingers and spring-backed thumb open as if caught in the act of grasping, tearing, rending. Will smiled.

The woman regained her composure and met his eyes with an embarrassed smile. "Be ready in a minute. What kinda pie you want?"

"Apple if you have it."

Surprise widened her eyes. "I think all the pies are frozen!"

"Don't worry about it, then."

When the coffee was ready she brought the pot over and filled his cup. Outside the wind whined as if in fear and the sky had gone dark. "Looks like a bad one," she said, pausing to stare out the window before returning to the counter and setting the pot upon its heater. "Sure hope Sam gets here soon."

"He's coming to pick you up?" Will removed his gum and wrapped it in a serviette. Then he sipped slowly.

"Uh huh. From Billings. That's where I live."

It started snowing, the flakes spinning in the wind. Will stared at the jukebox for a moment, then frowned and nodded at the wrecks outside. "Pretty smashed up, that Bug."

"No kidding. That was just last spring, too. Two killed, from a graduation party." She stood behind the counter clutching a red, blue and white tea towel in both hands, her face looking vaguely troubled as she watched the snow coming down. "We get lotsa accidents around here. Every year three or four dead, though it seems to be getting worse. They bring all the wrecks here."

Now that he was no longer behind the wheel, Will could feel his muscles easing their grip on his bones. "It's machines," he muttered, then turned to face her. "Some people get that machine under them and they think they're God. Maniacs behind the wheel." He shook his head. "Makes you wonder what the country's coming to." He raised his cup to his lips.

"It's just meant to be," the woman said, her eyes unconsciously dropping to his prosthesis, then away without meeting his gaze. "People die because they were meant to."

"Makes you wonder," Will repeated, his brow clenching as if in the grip of threatening thoughts. Abruptly he shook his head, smiled at the woman who stood staring at him. "Me, I didn't die—I got this here arm instead." Chuckling, he faced the storm again.

"Want more coffee?" she asked after a moment.

"Sure. Why not get off your feet and pour yourself one while you're at it." He sensed her hesitation. "Got anything good on that jukebox?" He smiled at her. "Probably not. Probably just Rock'n Roll. That's all you young people listen to nowadays."

The woman shook her head. "Not me. I'm a country fan. Most of my friends are, too." Carrying the pot over she set it down on the table and sat down. "The selection's not so good on that thing. All these people I never heard of." She shrugged, then after a moment asked, "What kinda stuff you usually pull in that thing?"

Will drew his left arm back, let it rest on his lap under the table so she'd stop trying to avoid staring at it. "Machine parts. Got a whole load

4

Machines

to drop off. Tons of parts." Taking the pot he filled her cup then his own.

"You mean that's what you're going to pick up."

"No that's what I'm carrying."

When he looked up she was staring at him strangely, then she turned away, reaching for the sugar. "What's your name, if you don't mind my asking?"

"Will Offstead."

"My name's Doris Havershank." Her eyes fell to the cup cradled in her hands, then out the window. "See that yellow Ford? I knew the guy who was killed in that. He was a friend of my brother." She smiled at him. "I guess you see alotta accidents, hey?"

Will nodded.

"You married?"

"Was. She died ten years ago."

The snow was coming down heavily now; he couldn't even see the road. He'd be lucky if he made it into Billings. A drift had gathered around the wrecked Bug.

"You want to hear some music? There's some not-so-bad stuff in there, I guess." She made as if to rise, but Will held up his hand.

"No. No, I don't." He met her surprised stare briefly, then looked down at the table. "I don't like music much. Used to, but not anymore." He scowled at himself, shook his head. There was silence in the cafe except for the rattle of the heater.

"Nice rig you got out there," Doris said, gazing at it. "What's her name?"

"Ahab's Ghost. A friend of mine gave me that name. Said it was from some old book. Never read it myself."

"My brother lost two fingers—stuck them in a combine. And my grandfather got his foot blown off in World War I. But he hated to read."

Staring at his empty cup, Will remained silent. His thoughts had suddenly grown dark.

The wind moaned and shook the door briefly, then fell away as if circling the building for another way inside. Doris gave an exaggerated shiver and smiled when he lifted his eyes to her face. "Yep, I seen alotta accidents. How about you? You been in many?"

"Only one." Will replied dully, his stomach twisting in a knot.

"Only one?" Her eyes flicked down to the tabletop that hid his mechanical arm, as if she could see right through the formica and wood.

"Naw," Will lifted his left arm slightly. "I lost this to cancer."

"Was it a bad accident? The one you were in?"

Meeting her wide and empty gaze he suddenly wanted to snarl at her, fill those rabbit eyes with terror. Instead, he nodded, feeling the tightness creeping back into him. "It was back east," he paused, "On a freeway just outside New York. This guy in a VW Bug pulled out from the slow lane right into mine." He felt like pleading but savagely fought it back. "He wasn't doing more than thirty, and I was doing sixty." His hand encircled the chipped cup on the table in front of him. "I never seen anything like it. My truck just ate that thing up and spat it back out—a chewed up burning heap. Killed him instantly. It wasn't my fault, everyone agreed, there were a hundred witnesses. It made the national news." With a flick of his finger he toppled the cup and watched as the few remaining drops trickled out. "He was a famous singer. I'd never heard of him, never heard anything he'd done."

Staring at the spilled coffee as if it was blood, Will did not look up as Doris stood and slowly walked over to the counter. She returned with her white, blue and red rag, sat down, lifted the cup and wiped up the mess. Raising his head, Will turned his gaze into the shadows where the jukebox squatted.

"And I never seen his name in any jukebox."

"Who was he?"

Standing up, Will shrugged. "Coulda been anyone." He hesitated, frowning, then walked over to the jukebox.

"That box is full of nobodies," Doris said dismissively.

"Yeah, nobodies." Standing in front of the machine he ran his gaze down the list of names behind the glass. It was dark, and the glass showed more of his face than the songs beneath it. It didn't surprise him when he found the name. "He's here," he said dully. "He's on the list." He pointed numbly, as a child might at an open casket funeral, then, suddenly feeling foolish, he made a fist and struck the jukebox.

"Hey! Don't do that!"

Will ignored her. He could feel his muscles tauten around his neck like a noose, making his breath shallow and raspy, cutting off the flow of blood until his face grew hot. Reaching into a pocket he searched for a coin, a part of him afraid, terrified at the thought of hearing that dead voice filling the empty cafe. "It wasn't my fault," he whispered. Stepping around the box he bent down to look for the cord.

"Was he a rock star?" Doris stood behind him; he could feel her presence like a weight pressing down on his back.

"What if he was?" he snapped in reply as he found the cord and plugged it into the wall. A whir thrummed in the jukebox and the lights flashed on, filling the glass. Will dropped a quarter in the slot and then stopped.

It was madness. It wouldn't mean a thing, just an empty voice, a ghost voice mocking everything that was still alive. It wasn't worth it, and it wasn't his fault.

Facing Doris, he hissed, "Why's he here?" Full of accusation and hurt he glared at her. "For months I looked—in every damn jukebox I seen, and he wasn't in any of them. Why here?"

Mutely, Doris shook her head.

Will studied her pudgy face. The makeup was smeared beneath her watery eyes as if to make her gaze older and wiser, but it wasn't. Her lipstick was uneven, cracked by the dry air. She breathed loudly through her mouth. Her mousy hair fell in strings to her round shoulders, tangled with lost and hopeless dreams. She shifted her hips, leaning on one leg then the other in a broken mime of uncertainty.

Christ, he muttered, what would she know? Scowling, Will spun around and punched in the letter and number. He waited, nothing happened.

Doris gasped. "Oh! I think it's broken! I think it broke a while ago."

Will's shoulders slumped. He took a deep breath, paused, then walked around to the left side of the jukebox. Gripping one end with his right hand, he clamped his metal fingers down at the other end. "Maybe its just jammed." He rocked it back and forth, harder and harder. The steel claws slipped and his left arm shot forward as the box rocked back against the wall. There was a loud crunch.

7

"Oh!"

Swearing, Will freed his arm, held it before him and examined the damage. The plastic flesh had shattered, revealing the rods, pins and springs of the inner mechanism. He flexed it. "It's just the shell. Just the outside—everything inside's okay." He smiled at her. "It's fine."

Doris stared as if he had just slit his wrist, her mouth gaping.

"I said it's fine!" Will snapped, pulling it away. Plastic shards spilled out and fell to the floor. Will bent down and gathered the pieces, dropped them into his pants pocket. After a moment he turned and faced the jukebox. "Christ, what's this country coming to?"

Headlights flashed in the window and Doris whirled. "It's Sam! He's come to pick me up."

Will nodded. "Yeah, I'd best be going. Gotta make it into Billings by tonight." They walked back to the table and he put on his jacket. "How much do I owe you?"

The door opened and an old man walked in amidst a flurry of snow. Pulling off his gloves he nodded at Will. "Evening. Nice rig you got out there."

"He just came in for a coffee," Doris explained, then said to Will: "That'll be fifty cents."

Sam waved his gloves, walked past them towards the counter. "Forget it. Don't bother, Dorry. Coffee's free on a night like this."

"Thanks," Will replied. "Well, gotta drop off my load. I'll be seeing you, and thanks again."

"Drop it off?" Sam laughed from behind the counter. "You better pick it up first!" He laughed again.

"What're you talking about?" Will buttoned his coat with one hand, faced the door. "Gotta whole load of machine parts on right now. What are you, snowblind?" He laughed and stepped out into the storm.

In the cab of the Kenworth, Will stared at the wrecked VW Bug, at the snow that lay heaped around it. That damn burnt rubber taste returned to his mouth and he reached for his packet of Beeman's. Muttering, he checked all three mirrors, but the storm had turned them all black. He couldn't see a damn thing back there.

This Rich Evil Sound

I'M NOT an old man. Sometimes the tracks old men think along are so deep cut nobody can see where they're going, maybe not even them. But then I think that maybe there are different kinds of old. People say I should've been born a hundred years ago. Does that make me old in some way?

They don't mean harm when they talk like that. It's just that they don't know me. I was in love with this girl, once, back in high school. Her name was Linda, and she was pretty popular, I guess. One day in the lunchroom I got down on one knee and sang for her a love song. One of my buddies had laid a dare on me—they sat at their table laughing and cheering. It was something I wanted to do anyway. No harm in it. The guys thought it was silly, but that's all right, too.

I know people make fun of me. I just look at things different from others. Before I got big I used to get in fights. There's always guys who don't like the way you look at things. They think it makes you weaker than them, maybe, and that's what they were trying to prove by fighting me. By the time I was fifteen they left me alone. They still figured me weak in my head, probably, but my body didn't look weak, not anymore.

I'm twenty now, so people have been leaving me alone for about five years. I don't mind. I like being alone. I quit school when I was sixteen, headed out into the bush. I spent the winter in northern Manitoba, nearly froze my feet off. I learned to lay trap lines from this Ojibwa Indian. He didn't know a word of English, except "nineteen seventy." I tried to teach him "nineteen eighty," because that was the year, but I don't think he ever got it. When I got back to Winnipeg I applied for and got a trapping license and that's what I've been doing ever since, out in Whiteshell Park.

In summers the park is full of people, so I head to Grassy River where it's quieter. But in the winter the only people in the park are rangers and trappers and old people who don't like the city and stay in their cabins. I don't mind running into those people, because we usually look at things the same way, and they don't make fun of me or anything.

This winter I was working Redrock Lake and the Whiteshell River. I'd heard from one of the rangers that Charlie Clark was wintering for the first time up at his cottage on Jessica Lake, so I decided to pay him a visit. Ever since they'd retired, Charlie and his wife had been spending the summers out here. But his wife died last summer, so he was all alone. I knew he'd be glad for some company.

I use a tent, but most trappers got cabins, because the years just pull at you and pretty soon a tent or quincy's too cold. It gets hard checking the lines when all your bones ache. Charlie wasn't a trapper, but I knew he'd understand and put me up for a couple days so I could dry out and get toasty. I'm pretty tough but I don't mind some luxury when I can get it.

Getting to Jessica Lake was easy. The Whiteshell River connects most of the lakes in the park. I broke camp an hour before dawn and walked the river. Winter's the quietest season. You're the only thing moving, the only thing making any sound. You listen to your breath, to the backpack creaking in its straps, to the crunch of your snowshoes. You can sing songs to pass the time and your voice sounds beautiful. And you can think about things, taking all the time you want to, with nobody pushing you for answers. You can think as slow as you like, and the rest of the world, if it cares at all, just waits. No ticking clocks, just shadows all blue and soft and moving slower than you can see.

I reached the park highway by noon. They keep it ploughed for the cross-country skiers who come out from Winnipeg on warm weekends and for people like Charlie Clark.

I smelled woodsmoke long before I saw his cottage. There'd been a cold snap the last couple weeks. No snow, no wind, just that rich silence under a sun-dogged sky. The smoke hung in the air like it had no place to go, smelling bittersweet because it was black spruce. It's not a good wood to burn, since it goes fast and doesn't give off much heat. I figured Charlie was getting low on his wood supply. A few minutes later the cottage came into view, its windows lit.

I gave a shout just to warn him, then turned into the driveway. At the porch I unstrapped my snowshoes. Charlie had came to the window and was now trying to open the frozen door. He had to shove it hard a couple times before it swung free of its frame.

"Goddammit, Daniel, it's good to see you! Get in here!"

"You running low on wood, Charlie?" I asked as I stepped inside and Charlie closed the door behind me.

"Just one pile's getting down," Charlie said. "I cleared some black spruce from out back last summer. Just using it up. How the hell have you been?"

"Good." I took my backpack off, started stripping down some. "Thick pelts this winter."

Charlie shook his head, rubbing his brow. "Animals. They always know when it's gonna be a cold one. They always know, don't they?"

"Sure do," I said. We went into the den and sat down in front of the fireplace. The ranger had told me that Charlie had taken his wife's death pretty hard, and I could see that he didn't look too good. The skin of his face was pasty and yellow. And I saw that a shaking had come to his hands. "How you been, Charlie?" I asked, stretching my feet towards the fire.

"Strange winter, eh?" Charlie looked down, rubbing his forehead again. "I know this sounds funny, but I'm tasting metal these days." He squinted at me. "Can't really explain it, Daniel. But ever since the snows hit for real, I might as well be eating lead ten times a day, from the taste I'm tasting."

I glanced at him, then looked away. He was giving me this real troubled look. I stared at the fire. "Don't know," I finally said. "Maybe it's the lake water."

"Hell no, it isn't like that." He paused. "Had a heart attack last summer, did you know that?"

I shook my head. "Didn't hear anything about it. How bad was—"

"The doctor in the city—I forget his name, he took over when Bill retired, just a kid, really—he's been phoning me about once a week, asking me how I'm doing. So I tell him, but he says it's just psychological.

He says there's no way somebody can taste a pacemaker. I suppose he knows what he's talking about." Charlie looked up at me and smiled. "But he was the one making the connection with the wind-up, not me, right? I just said to him, 'I keep tasting metal, Doc. How about that?' "

"And what did he say to that?"

"Psychological, like I told you."

"Oh yeah. Right." I studied the flames, listened to the snapping wood. It was burning real fast, that black spruce. For some reason I wanted it to slow down. It was burning too fast, just eating itself up and hardly any warmth reaching my feet. The way the wood spit out sparks bothered me, too, like words coming so quick all you can do is nod, answering everything "yes" no matter what you hear.

"Young people," Charlie said. "The ones in the city, like that doc." He looked at me. "The city people—can you figure them, Daniel?"

I laughed. "If I could maybe I wouldn't be here."

"You can't figure them, then?"

I shrugged. "They're just different, that's all. Like when things go quiet—they gotta make noise. So when they do something funny everybody laughs real loud, and it's not quiet anymore, and they get comfortable again. And winter, and the bush—well, they don't know what winter is, and they don't like the bush, the way it just swallows their noise. You couldn't laugh loud enough to keep that from happening, I bet."

Charlie was nodding. "Always questions, that's what I notice. Always 'why?' They ask 'why?' and then they answer themselves right away. 'Why?' 'Because.' Just like that. Making everything seem so simple. Know what I mean? And they're always so suspicious, especially about complicated things, like when I say I'm tasting metal. 'Why?' 'Psychological.' Just like that. I was a teacher, did you know that, Daniel?"

"Sure."

"Ten-year-old kids like that question. 'Why?' How old are you, Daniel?"

"Twenty," I said, feeling uncomfortable for some reason, maybe about the way he kept using my name. He made it sound strange, like it wasn't my own. I thought about what I'd said, about city people, and I wondered at how angry I got saying it.

Charlie was talking. "Me and Mary couldn't have kids, did you know that? It was a hard thing for her to accept. I didn't mind. I didn't mind at all. The Lord just didn't see fit, that's all."

The room should have felt cozy, with the bear rug between us and all the knick-knacks crowding the shelves, the mounted jack and the antlers on the walls, the easy chair deep and comfortable. But it didn't feel cozy. I put more black spruce on the fire, then pulled my chair closer to it. "Anybody else drop by?" I asked.

Charlie nodded. "Yeah, the strangest winter. And it's not just the taste in my mouth, either. When it was snowing the ploughs used to come and clear the road a couple times a week. I'd go out and give them a wave, let them know I haven't run out of batteries or something." He laughed. "On the really cold days I flagged them down, gave them a thermos of hot chocolate. And you know, no matter if it was a different driver next week, I always got the thermos back. Sometimes we talked a bit. You know, just to keep the jaws greased. I told them about the buck, the one that comes across the lake every morning, right up to the cabin looking for food. And the very next week one of the drivers drops off two bales of hay. How about that?"

He'd been talking so fast I wondered if I'd missed something. "Charlie, what buck?"

He looked surprised. "I didn't tell you about the buck?"

"I don't think so."

Charlie's gaze returned to the fire. "Hasn't snowed in weeks. The ploughs stopped coming. Sometimes I swear I can hear them, way off down the road, so I go out, right? I go out and wait, figuring they're coming to check up on me. But they must be doing something else, cause they don't come. I can hear them, all right. They must be busy, right?"

"Sure." I stood. "Listen, I'm gonna get some other wood, if that's all right?"

"Fine. You go right ahead and get it, Daniel. That's fine by me. I got some birch out back."

"Great," I said.

Outside, I stood in front of the woodpile, holding Charlie's axe in my hands. I listened to the silence beyond the sounds of my breath. The muscles around my neck felt tight. I let the quiet sink into me, studied the grey trees beyond the clearing. Without leaves the trees all seemed to be standing alone, each one cut off from the others. The snow beneath them was like empty space, as if the roots and earth had been wiped away, leaving nothing behind.

My feet began to tingle. My toes had been frozen so many times there wasn't much feeling left in them anyway. All I had to do, I knew, was to get moving, but I just kept standing there, and the cold started working its way up my legs the way it does—picking out little areas, making them feel sort of wet, exposed. Then the feeling goes and there's just an empty patch. My knees went, then my thighs.

Behind me the backdoor opened. "Hey, Daniel?"

The spell, or whatever it was, broke. I turned around. Charlie was standing just inside the door, clouds of vapor around his legs. "Just thinking," I said to him, smiling.

"Thought you froze right up!" Charlie said, laughing. "Hurry up back inside. I got hot chocolate brewing."

"Right," I said, turning back to the woodpile. I began pulling out birch logs. To split them all I had to do was let the axe fall of its own weight—the logs seemed to almost jump apart. But the moving around brought the feeling back to my legs.

I piled wood on the back porch, then brought an armload inside. Charlie was in the kitchen, standing by the stove.

"They must be pretty busy, right?" he asked, stirring Fry's cocoa into a pot of simmering milk.

"Who?"

"The guys who clear the roads, like I was saying before. There's lots of side roads that probably need work, ones they couldn't get around to earlier, right? Can you believe this cold snap? All night long I can hear trees cracking. Exploding, you know? It's an eerie sound, all right. Can't say I like it. Do you like it, Daniel? I've been getting up at dawn and I make some coffee and sit in the rocker so I can look out over the lake.

"That's how I first saw the buck, looking out over the lake. He comes from the far side, every morning. Stumbling through the deep snow. Uses a different trail every time. Can you figure that?"

Charlie poured us cups of hot chocolate. We returned to the den. I set my cup down on the mantle and went to bring in the birch. The echo of the axe splitting the wood kept going through my head, making me think of what Charlie had been saying about exploding trees.

I stoked the fire, then sat down again. "That doc in the city," I said, "he's still phoning you every week?"

Charlie rubbed his face, then licked his lips. "I unplugged the phone. He kept saying the same old thing, over and over again." He leaned towards me and gestured for me to get closer. "Tell me, do you think my tongue's turning blue?" He poked out his tongue.

I looked at it, then sat back. "Hard to tell," I said. "Don't think so."

"I think so," Charlie said.

The heat coming from the birch logs made me push my chair back. I thought about the nights I'd spent alone, wrapped in my Woods arctic sleeping bag, watching my breath lay a sheet of ice on the nylon ceiling above me. I'd be filled with the silence, so filled and warm, with my thoughts going slow as they like to do. Then crack! A tree would explode. I'd jump, stare into the darkness, my heart pounding. Black spruce. It's the black spruce that explodes.

"I hope the ploughs come back," Charlie said. "We're running low on hay." He frowned suddenly. "Oh," he said, "I forgot." He climbed to his feet. "Come on, Daniel, let's look out over the lake."

I followed him to the large frosted window. We stood side by side and stared outward. I could see the buck's trails, shadowed blue. They stopped at a scuffed-up area just below the porch deck, maybe thirty feet away. The scuffed-up area was spattered with frozen blood, and off to one side lay the frosted carcass of the buck, half eaten.

"Wolves? Jesus, nobody's seen a wolf in this park for years."

Charlie asked, "Did you see the Northern Lights last night?"

"I'm usually asleep by seven," I said.

"From horizon to horizon, I've never seen them so big. They made a sound like, like wind on sand, falling all around. All around. It's so beautiful, Daniel. There's no real way to describe it, is there?"

"Not really. You're right in that." But I knew that sound, the voice behind the silence, the voice that pushed the silence into me. And I knew

15

what that voice said, the single word over and over again. Alone, alone, alone.

"Only," Charlie continued, "only, there'd be this falling from the sky, right? And all these streams of colour. And deep in the forest, deep in the forest, Daniel. The trees kept on shattering. As if, for just last night, for just those few hours when I was standing out there, the world was made of glass. The thinnest glass. And the trees reaching upward. I don't know." Charlie turned to me, a terrible frown on his lined face. "Maybe the trees were made of glass, too. But all gnarled and bubbled and black. Trying to join the sky, but too rough." He turned back to the window. "Too rough. Just no way they could make it. They were reaching up, to where the colours played. Reaching. Then snapping. Like gunshots. I tell you, in certain lights you can see it—the blue on my tongue. Then the glass in the sky shattered, and there was this falling. Endless falling."

I nodded. "Like the world was made of glass." His words had left a pain inside me, a deep, spreading pain. "Too rough," I said, "wanting to play with the colours, all the colours. But too rough." The voice whispered its word in my head, and it hurt me.

"That buck," Charlie said, "he was so strong, so healthy. All his life. You could see that. He—I built this cabin with my own hands, Daniel, did you know that? He was strong, healthy. He'd been through hard times lately, but he was all right. Four wolves. I watched it all happen. That buck, running across the lake, full bore. I was sitting in this rocker, this one right here. They took him not twenty yards from here—you can see where he first went down. I'd been thinking about getting my bear rifle, but it was already too late. That's the way it looked anyway. But the buck," he shook his head, "that buck, he just got up and kept coming. You can see it—he dragged those wolves ten, fifteen yards. Dragged all of them."

"Son of a bitch," I said.

"He'd been so strong, all his life. He dragged them all right, but in the end it didn't matter. It didn't count for nothing. I just sat here, all this morning, watching them wolves eating. Funny, they kept walking around and around him, not knowing what to do, really. What to do with it all."

I stared at the carcass, at the gnawed ribs and purple ice-flecked meat.

"They'll be back for more," I said. "They earned it."

"I'm thinking, Daniel, the same things over and over again. Funny how that happens, eh? I'm thinking about my rifle, and that taste filling my mouth. Metal. He'd been so strong, cut down just like that. And I'm thinking about this window, this one right in front of us, Daniel. Two panes each a quarter inch thick. How everything happened in absolute silence. And the only sound I knew, I know, is something I feel more than hear. It's probably psychological, eh, Daniel? But there's this tingling, like glass chimes, and there's this humming—both coming from my chest. It's fading, I think, Daniel."

I shook my head, again and again, but he wasn't paying any attention to me. I didn't even know what I was saying no to, but in my head a voice kept asking, "Why?" Why? And Charlie, he kept answering me, he kept saying "Because, Daniel. Only because. Just because."

"The strangest winter," Charlie said. "No way to explain it, any of it. My tongue turning bluer and bluer, getting stained deeper and deeper every time, the doc telling me it's psychological—what the hell is that supposed to mean?"

We stood there for a long time, staring at the carcass. I wanted to cry, I wanted to shut my ears, stop the silence outside, never again let it in. But the tracks were cut too deep inside me. I'm not an old man. I don't think I'm very smart as far as young people go. I was never good at things they're good at. I'm not brave, and I'm sorry for that. I really am. I left Charlie that afternoon. I ran from him, across the lake, using one of the buck's trails. I pitched my tent on the other side of Jessica Lake. I could've gone farther but I didn't. I know it wasn't a tree shattering that woke me that night, made me jump up, staring into the darkness, heart pounding. I know that it wasn't a tree, and I'm sorry. Truly sorry.

Better Places to Be

CANDER STOOD at the window, clothed only in darkness. She studied her reflection, the paleness of it, the places men found desirable. Full breasts, the slight bulge of her tummy, the indent at her neck. Mammary glands, some fat, and the gap between clavicles. A reduction of the intangible into cold nomenclature. She worked it like a ritual.

Smoke drifted from her nostrils, rolling up the window pane in the vent's hot updraft. Weight on one leg, angling full hips, elbow perched on folded arm, cigarette tip burning a hole in her cheek's reflection.

All of it, all of her superimposed on the city, the city beyond the sleet-crusted balcony, the city squatting beneath a pink sky crazed with whirling snow. A few towers rose into the maelstrom, but not enough to alter the way the city seemed to huddle against the earth, shoulders hunched to the winter wind.

The beast in the bed behind her whined softly, shifting under sweat-soaked sheets. A wolf, but maybe just a dog. No full moon involved in this, just a simple denigration into maudlin whimpering. Predictable. A man a few hours ago, now something else, something less.

Cander tried to like the thought. A sense of power would be good right now. She needed an answer to what had happened earlier in the evening. An answer not to some mystery, but to a nagging, gnawing helplessness. But trying wasn't working. She'd broken him, and felt broken herself.

She stared down at the city, at its blurred lights of life. A deception. Electric activity, nothing more. Mindless and perfect. Lights of life without life. Feeling helpless had become such a habit. Same for the way she answered it. Her gaze focused again on her reflection. Without life, but look at all the blood she'd spilled. Must come from somewhere, some pumping thing, vulnerable to human pain. Not from a wolf, not from a dog. From a man. From this man.

Everything had changed. She knew too many of her own secrets.

Soft yellow light bathed the legislature building a half mile away. Domed like some corporate mosque, with a golden boy on the run, perched with torch in hand. Evolved from gargoyles, from the winged demons that even now circled, hunting the homeless—a golden boy, weren't they all.

The season's first storm. A night that demanded a nasty, violent ending. Killing off the embarrassments, the victims. She'd done her part, with style.

But now she wasn't sure. He was hidden under her sheets. He could be anybody, he could be the one she'd wanted—still wanted.

The beast grunted in its sleep. Cander lit another cigarette, studying the act in this thin, uncertain mirror, her eyes finding themselves through the smoke. Such a defiant, studied gesture, and behind it all swirled the endless snow.

*

The city's heart was stone. Cut from famous quarries, the limestone was prison to contortions, demonic conjurings that had once been alive. A heart infused with mineralized bones and shell, with cilia and spiral ducts, worm tracks and columns of coral. Like cold tomb walls, the heiroglyphics of extinction.

The figures hunching against them, wrapped in swaths of ragged clothing, had their heads bent close, as if intent on cracking the code, as if listening to ghostly voices whispering dissolution and urging the impervious promise of stone over weak flesh.

The scene beyond the cab's window seemed endless. Some modern fool's caryatid chorus line. Tonight's storm would kill dozens. Heeding the call, flesh turning rigid, brittle. Flesh into stone. Personal extinctions with no one to grieve.

Inside the cab it was warm.

"Nobody wants to know about the past," Severan was saying, his eyes catching streetlamps, water-blurred irony.

"What about us?" Luscia demanded. "Aren't we interested?"

"Interested, but not interesting."

19

He was good at this, Cander reflected, wondering if what she was feeling was envy. Luscia had commented on the street people, some sympathetic murmer that came from anywhere but compassion. Cander mused on what it would be like living on the surface, like Luscia. A leaf of opinion flung about on unseen currents of emotion. The origin of every thought a mystery.

Severan had responded with an obscure reflection on the past. Somehow, he never commented on what Luscia said, but unerringly spoke to those invisible currents that tugged her.

Severan—Severan had no surface. None Cander could see, anyway.

The cab turned onto a side street, some shortcut between sagging tenements looking garish and atavistic. Too many details, too few straight lines. Nothing of today's austere ethic.

"It's dying all around us," Severan said.

Cander glanced at the cabbie's face in the mirror. Black as the nightsky, yellow eyes.

"They should tear all this down," Luscia said.

"I live around here," Severan said.

Luscia's eyes widened. "Why?"

Cander wondered about the three of them in this cab—no, four, including the driver. Words like performances in an elevator full of strangers. And the silent listeners. Just one mare artificial construct, a modern abridgement of culture and class. It didn't feel real.

"Why not?" Severan said. "This is where policy finds its last face. And lo, it's ravaged. Pits, scars and despair, Luscia."

"You' re just slumming."

Cander said, "No he isn't." Severan never got angry—when she was around she did it for him. "He's poor." She'd needed no emphasis on that word. Deliver it flat, blunt enough to silence Luscia. An alien, turbulent word for Luscia.

Severan shifted, looked out his window. Cander watched his reflection. A momentary smile, then, "I don't drink or do drugs. I barely watch television. Nothing to blur the bars of my cage."

"Nothing's keeping you here, Severan," Luscia said. A dismissal.

"The poor are dumb, the dumb are poor," Severan said, nodding.

"Absolutely. A state of mind. I don't belong because I can do better, right? Got it."

"You want pity?"

"No. I want out."

"Then do it. Just get out."

Severan was silent for a moment. Then he said, "Okay."

Luscia wasn't buying. She snorted, crossing her arms and tightening up, as if they cramped her on both sides—Severan's quiet bitterness and Cander's stiff anger. Luscia built quick walls, very austere.

"We're dead and dying and nobody notices," Severan continued, his tone level and detached. "We keep stepping out of each other's way. A headlong flight. But I'm not being original here, am I?"

"I know about poverty," Luscia said, diffident. "In Puerto Rico—

"Case studies, huh? Look at Max here, behind the wheel in our cozy cab. Five years ago he was on the run in Haiti."

Luscia seemed startled, but quickly recovered. "Meaning?"

"Meaning look at him now."

The cabbie's head bobbed. "I'm alive, Walker."

"Good to know, since you're driving." Severan scratched the old scar on his forehead, the one he'd brought back with him from Central America—a subconscious gesture that hinted of rites of passage. "So, Luscia, what's changed? Max and I drink coffee at the same cafe. Almost the same hours. Only we never sit together. Max sits with his fellow refugees and I sit alone, listening in on their conversations. What's changed. He's not just some black guy hoping for a good tip anymore, is he, Luscia?"

"What's your point?"

"My point is," Severan said, "I could've kept my mouth shut."

*

The next ten minutes in silence. They left the rotting core for the strip that ran straight to the university. Bars and gas bars, the sidewalks empty like some abandoned mode of transport, neon everywhere.

Cander leaned back in the seat and closed her eyes. Case studies. Poverty in Haiti. Turgid statistical analyses in a dry, superior tone—superior as in tears of sympathy but leave my wallet alone, Severan had said once, in class. Professor Marcus Romanow threw a full cup of coffee at him. When they finally arrived, Luscia paid. A ten-dollar tip.

*

Cander glanced around, counting the men she'd slept with. All the women who despised her. She made her private smile public.

Cordially invited. Students welcome, except sluts that fucked for marks. Sluts ignored.

Severan gave her a grin. He went one way, Luscia pointedly another. Cander reached for a cigarette, feeling eyes on her. All that pain, all that betrayal.

She'd taken in the faculty lounge at a glance. Rectangular, white-walled, five sets of sofas squared off, backs to the open spaces like Roman forts. Storage rooms had been emptied for the occasion, artifacts dusted off and now in prominant display on tabletops, shelves in glass cases and elegant cabinets. Pots with grimacing faces, masks and implements, cups, mortars and pestles, costumes, head dresses and dolls.

Foodstuffs held position on a long table off to one side. Olives and smoked salmon with toothpick spears. The bar opposite, a wheeled contraption like a gurney for the lame and desperate. An undergrad stood behind it, attaching plastic cups to stems when not serving drinks.

Counting the men she'd slept with—burned out professors and promising grad students. Still a man's world. The few women among them so bristling with armor as to be indistinguishable, not a single feminine gesture among them.

A man's world. Cander delivered punishment, and she did it seriously. What they thought of her was nothing compared to what she thought of them, and their thoughts came later, long afterward. Hers came under the sheets. Giving, then taking away. Hah hah and fuck you, little man.

She felt the bitch in her come alive. A rush of power. Severan admired it, or so he'd said once. She wondered what he'd be like in bed, and knew she'd never know. A friend—a word she didn't use often, a word that scared her—that's what he was. Cander never fucked her friends.

"Want to see my trophy collection?"

She turned. "Hi, Max." Another Max, a different Max, pink skinned, white eyes behind granny glasses, a Max never on the run. Bitch lingering, she waved carelessly at the crowd. "You're looking at mine. Care to compare notes?"

A pained expression, bless him.

"Never mind," she said lightly, following it with a laugh. "Let's get a drink."

As they headed to the bar, Max took her arm in his. Always a surprise, the way her friends responded to who she was—protective, as if they knew she'd never bother protecting herself. Even more surprising, it never annoyed her. Some responses were just too instinctual, too genuine to be shoved into a political arena.

"What are we doing here?" Max asked softly, almost in disbelief. "I hate these people."

She nudged her elbow into him. "This is anthropology, Max. These are anthropologists. They're all talking at once because observation's their business."

"Well, I saw Severan back there, chatting up the department head. I don't know, maybe they're secret bridge partners—who can tell these days."

"Severan playing the game? I don't believe it."

"My own eyes, Candy."

"If you'd heard him earlier in the cab. Getting under Luscia's skin—she's hopeless sometimes. But when he said he wanted out, he meant it."

They reached the bar.

"What, no beer?" Max pulled off his glasses and glared at the bartender. "No beer? The very lifeblood of European civilization, and you don't have any?"

Cander took a glass of red wine and left Max berating the freshman bartender. Max was big on initiation rites.

Hunting up a conversation wasn't going to be easy, she knew. All her histories here were bloody, and the ones keeping the most distance were the ones who'd only heard things second hand. She strolled across the room, slipping a sway into her hips, wishing the wine was cheaper than it tasted. Her clothes already announced civilization's end run, virgin to whore in three easy years. Every man's fantasy come true, too true—

their vision of the whore always came through gauze, lace, a soft lense. They never expected the grime, the sweat, the historical facts.

Romanticism was rife in anthropology—one of Severan's clinical observations, voiced mockingly from an armchair a few months back at some deadly basement-suite gathering of grad students, smell of stale smoke and beer—parties that bred like spores of despair, she couldn't remember which one it'd been. An observation worth remembering, though Cander's private slant was more cynical than clinical. He kept people at a distance. She brought them too close.

Cander felt ready for another victim, an innocent to stab through the heart.

She slowed her stroll. Swinging a low predatory gaze across the room was something she'd practised to perfection. Get the hairs rising on their thick necks, the game's afoot. What I want none of you can give me. But I'll take what you've got.

Two more mouthfuls and the wine was gone. Ready for another. A face caught her eye, jarring her out of raptor mode, jarring her into a blankness that stopped her in her tracks. Max. Not the white Max. The black one, the cabbie. Just standing there. In a white stream chuckling to itself on all sides, a black rock. The yellow of his eyes like Caribbean cream, soft around dark coffee—eyes fixed on something across the room. Sweat glistened on his face, melted snow dripped from his pale leather jacket.

The shock opened her up suddenly, cranking up the volume of conversations all around her. Dissertations in full defense. "Maori—Innuit—Yanomano—Kiowa—Beaker People—Aurignacian—Upper Pleistocene—Dorset—Head Smashed In—Fort Dauphin—Levallois— Fifth Dynasty—" A barrage of otherness, a subtle seige on the here and now. A here and now rocked on its hinges, dented by this incongruity, this intrusion from the outer world.

The department head crossed Cander's line of sight, her face pale, eyes smouldering and fixed straight ahead. The old woman's anger cut a swath through the crowd, figures shrinking back as she headed for the coat rack beside the doors. Blankly, Cander's eyes followed the woman for a moment. When she looked back, Max was gone. On the wall where he'd been standing leered a Haida mask.

Conversations roaring. Noise like so much noise, waves rising, bouncing, filling every available space. Cander shook her head, the harsh movement almost making her reel. The wine? No, just the noise. A civilization of talkers talking loud to keep above the other talkers keeping above the rattle of radiators, mouths chewing dainty foodstuffs, a car engine in the roundabout outside, the flap of doors, chairs creaking—and some guy off to her left shouting like he was ready for a fight. She looked over to observe the ruckus and found Luscia at her side.

"What's got Marcus so pissed?" Luscia asked.

Another professor, Ingram, was forcefully holding Marcus back. Specialist in coca trade routes in Peru, Marcus was glaring at someone Cander couldn't see. Face red as a betel nut. His friends closed around him like musk oxen, but facing the wrong way—asses out—with stern glances over their shoulders. Defensive cordon without the hair and horns. Cander laughed. "Look at those old farts, where's my .303? Pathetic and bewildered, they deserve extinction."

"What?"

A man standing near the crowd caught Cander's attention. A Native. He looked lost, wearing a jack shirt over a thick woollen sweater. A pine-handled gaff hung from his belt. He kept nervous eyes on the scrum of professors. Cander's frown deepened.

"Who's that?" Luscia asked.

"The aborigine."

"Aborigine," Cander repeated slowly. "First People but not people first. Indigenous population. Treaty/non-Treaty, stipulate status and origin and sign here. Wait till your number's called."

"Candy? You all right?"

The Native was heading across the room, purposefully.

"He's got a gaff hook," Cander said.

"Oh God," Luscia whispered.

The man disappeared into a crowd, re-emerged unscathed and unnoticed. He came to the wall, reached up and collected the Haida mask.

Something muffled the conversations around Cander. The rush of her blood. She watched the Native cross the room again, push open the inner doors, pause in the foyer, tuck the mask under one arm and don gloves and hat. Then out into the night, into the swirling snow. Gone.

The scrum was breaking up. Tense shoulders slumping, outward glances numerically diminished. Heat dissipating.

"What's that smell?" Luscia asked.

"Testosterone."

"No, smells like curry. Candy, did that guy just steal that mask or what?"

"The Haida culture included ritual reciprocity. Maybe the mask's making the rounds. Off to find another white wall, off to leer at some other crowd. Maybe it's going home."

"So he stole it. Shouldn't we tell somebody?"

Cander shook herself, looked down at Luscia's tight, foundationed and rouged face, the eyes wide and lined with mascara. "Right. Where's Severan?"

Luscia shrugged. "Last I saw he was talking with Marcus."

Blinking, Cander said, "Really."

*

There would never be a gradual shift in power. For Cander, that realization came long ago. When the niches are already filled, you've got to bust ass to get a foothold. Rape the rapists. Loot the looters. Swell with the angry tide, sweep away what's past.

But beliefs were hard to shake. Panic stirred inside her. Never mind the cycles of the moon, Mazy slit the little lamb's throat and women have been cursed ever since. All the blood and semen she'd spilled into her toilet wasn't going to change that single gift from God.

There were other kinds of power, and its wresting away hurt. A dark-haired, dark-skinned, wiry little man wearing a blood-smeared apron stood at a cabinet, casually pocketing a half dozen artifacts from the Levant—clay figurines sculpted by refugees from Eden.

Everyone struggled not to notice, a fever of bewildered fear dimming the conversations, decibel by decibel. Increments of rising silence. Animated gesticulations diminished, mouths closing, faces drawing blank.

Cander searched the crowd, desperate for Severan. Detached and coolly amused, he'd have an answer to what was happening. She held to that thought with the hope of conviction, though in truth she already knew what was happening. She had her own personal analogy.

Max found them. His face whiter than usual, he took Cander's arm. "What's going on?" he asked.

"We should call the police," Luscia said.

They watched two Polynesian women in seamstress smocks struggle with a canoe prow, carefully extracting the carved figurehead from its stand. The women carried it between them to the doors.

Cander shook her head, pulling free of Max. "No. I can see it now. Cases held up in court for decades. Restitution." She shook her head again, searching for a cigarette. "Besides, this is just metaphor."

"I don't like the precedent," Max said.

"Of course you don't." She found her pack, set a cigarette between her lips. "It's a jarring recognition. We've all been romantics too long. And now we've been pushed out of our dream." She lit a match. "Cultural deconstruction, listen to what's left, listen to the growing silence." She brought the flame in for the kill.

Max seemed mesermized, his eyes tracking her every move.

Maybe he'd missed the shaking hand. Never mind. Cander scanned the crowd again. It was getting cold, the doors to the outside world opening again and again to someone carrying out an artifact of cultural and historical significance. Snow swirled in behind them, leaving white patches by the entrances that refused to melt.

She saw Severan. With Professor Neil Ingram, Ingram listening, Severan talking through a half smile.

Max nudged her. "Like I said, Candy." He sounded smug. "Playing the game."

*

"Sorcery," Severan was saying, his voice soft. "Some stranger's will conjuring the future, Jim. Squeal all you want, it's out of your hands. And mine." He paused. "I admire it, you know, the way we drown them with labels and segments and divisions of labour and love. We're so desperate about it, makes me wonder who's going to drown first."

27

Ingram, specialist in Caribbean religions, had gone from red to white. "You've been busy tonight," he said, his voice trembling. "You're on probation, Walker. And I swear I'll see you out on your ass within a week."

Severan laughed. "Probation. We're both on probation. Us pink pigmented pricks. Tell me, Jim, how come when we're left with ourselves we run out of things to say? Face it, we haven't been doing our job."

Ingram stared for a moment longer, then turned and walked away.

Severan faced Cander. "Don't stand so close."

She scowled. "I've heard of self-destructive but—"

"Have you? Looked in any mirrors lately? Never mind, we're all getting fucked, you've just turned the figurative into messy reality. How's it feel being a martyr?"

"What's got into you, Severan?" Max demanded, trying to move between them.

Cander firmly blocked him, her eyes searching Severan's.

"Is there a full moon, or what?" Luscia said, nervous and disgusted all at once.

Cander thought of possible answers, retorts, the nasty snick of knives opening, but something in Severan's face held her to silence. His face, only the face—his words had left her numb. Martyr?

Severan smiled wearily. "Metaphors are like euphemisms, Candy. They deserve dismantling. Keeps us from hiding too long." His smile softened. "Here all along you've been right in front of me. Showing me what's possible if you set your mind to it."

"That's right," Cander said. "I've set my mind to it."

"Expensive vengeance."

"Is it? Seems cheap compared to what you're doing."

He looked shocked. At a loss for words—she'd always wondered if she could do that to him. Once the bullshit was out of the way and she could call for help. She saw the growing dismay in his expression and wondered who'd won this contest of pain. It'd been a distant call. It would take time.

She gave him a winning smile. "You'd be surprised at what I can salvage." She left the three of them, ready to deck Max if he tried anything.

But he didn't. It was possible he didn't understand.

She sought out Ingram, the man who endlessly claimed to have once been possessed by a vodu spirit, serving the loa as only a nzambi can. That last bit had been Severan's, sotto voce. She stepped around an Innuit busy wrapping up a whalebone carving. Voices were dropping, ever dropping. It was hard not to notice, hard to pretend otherwise. The room was cold despite the groaning radiators. The white patches at the door had grown larger, an ice age of cultural dissent.

Ingram and Marcus huddled at the bar. Cander approached the narrow space between them, draped her arms over their shoulders and leaned in. A tit each, against their upper arms, deepening the already ample cleavage.

"Evening, gentlemen."

Breath hissed from Marcus, an expellation of old pain from between his teeth. She looked up into his red face and winked.

It was enough. He'd never needed much, she recalled. Marcus pulled back, away, mumbling a "hello" before making his escape. A marriage had gone down from that one. She took no responsibility. Merely making a point.

"It's been hard lately," Cander said, smiling as she swung close, giving him her body's full attention. Ingram was divorced and edging fifty. He had an ego that needed public displays. "Severan's struggling. No money, not much food. Still, I agree with the probation. He deserves it."

"Damn right he does," Ingram growled, tossing back his wine. "The little shit."

"And the best researcher we've got."

"Big fucking deal."

Ingram was getting drunk. The glance he finally threw at her was wild, hungry, but panicked. His pale eyes flicked away, searching over her shoulder, hardening. "We'll starve," he muttered. "Intellectual discourse turned into a vacuum. It's not like we aren't appreciative. Or respectful."

She felt like she'd missed something, concentrating too much on what she was about to do for Severan. She frowned. The man was whimpering, but he seemed on the edge of rage. "Respectful? Of what?"

He didn't respond. He was watching someone behind her, his body tensing dangerously.

"Neil? Let's get out of here."

"Diversity has to be recognized. We can't keep closing doors." He bared his teeth. "The bastard can't do this!"

Cander spun around, expecting to see Severan. But no. Max, the cabbie, Haitian on the run, was moving towards a display. Three votive dolls, Legba, Erzulie Freda and Ogoun, the spirits of Haiti. Ingram's own collection.

His heavy forearm shoved her aside. Cander stumbled, breaking a heel and falling to the carpeted floor. Ingram didn't even notice, marching to intercept the Haitian. Cander sat up, saw Severan sitting back in a chair near the display, his eyes on her. An expression she couldn't read.

"Candy!" The other Max, crouching beside her. His hands helping her up. "You okay?"

She wasn't sure. Something inside had been shaken loose—not a physical thing, something else. She felt small, humiliated. Treated like a whore.

"The bastard just pushed you—"

Cander kicked off her shoes, stepping free of her friend's grip. The other Max had reached the display. He opened the cabinet and stuffed Ogoun into his coat pocket.

"Leave them alone!" Ingram roared, the only voice in the room. He closed on Max like a linebacker.

At the last moment, Max stepped aside, impossibly lithe. Ingram crashed heavily into the cabinet. Wood splintered and the anthropologist sagged.

Max calmly collected the remaining two dolls. Without looking at anyone, he headed for the doorway.

Silence, every conversation dead in the cold air. Wind hissed with snow through the gaping doors.

Cander realized she was shaking. Beside her, Max stared at Ingram with something like pity. Cander studied her friend, the lines of his face and body. A shiver ran through her, and she took a sharp breath. "Max," she said softly.

He turned.

"I don't want to sleep alone tonight."

Max paled.

She took his arm.

*

It was near dawn, but still dark above the city. She'd chain-smoked half a pack. Even the demons above the legislature building were gone. There'd be dead in the streets, a nice Malthusian touch to the body politic's nature.

Severan was home, the bare-bulbed warren with the crumbs on the counter. Luscia was probably still out dancing, just one more ritual of possession.

Behind her he slept on. The white Max, the Max now on the run. She'd broken her rule, struggled the night through, seeking justification.

The white Max. Not what she wanted, not who she wanted, not an answer to this evening. An innocent victim, spoiling the metaphor. The white Max. The wrong Max.

The Brouhaha about Bill

ON A WINDING gravel road in Louisiana, shaded by Spanish moss and just north of a festering swamp, El Shoe lay flat out on his belly in the dust. The road dipped suddenly here, so it was the perfect place for an ambush. Somebody coming down the track wouldn't see anything amiss until it was too late.

Life's been good since humans showed up. El Shoe pumped his tongue to get the juices flowing, tried a few lazy blinks just to get the act down right in case some terrified flamingo was watching from the bushes.

Eating things is my job. I'm an alligator. I've been around a hundred million years, not a scale out of place and not one single, extra iota of brain matter added on since then, thank God. Who needs it?

I'm one mean bastard and I may be dumb as a duffel bag but I've got real big teeth, and take it from me, that's what counts in this world.

Small foreign cars packed with tourists, yummy morsels in loud clothing. They'll show up. I can wait. I can wait a thousand years, a million. I'm ready. I'm always ready. Just ask those stick-legged pink birds cowering in every bush. They're watching. I know it. I can feel it. They're in awe. Terrified. I'm an alligator, and I'm ready. Blink the lids. Pump the tongue. Look inconspicuous. Grease the jaw hinges, get them ready to open wide. Real wide.

*

Morning mist lay over the glade knee-high, which was damned inconvenient, Bill grumped as he cracked his shin against yet another black spruce stump. He stumbled a step forward and cracked another shin. He wobbled backward then to one side and double-whammied two more shins. Bill paused and counted. One, two, three, and four. Four shins.

That's right, he concluded.

Like all moose, Bill had trouble figuring out just how many legs he had at any one time. Every time he stopped for a count it came out at four. But that was no guarantee, was it? What if the fifth one was hiding somewhere. You could count four till you were blue in the face and it wouldn't prove a thing, would it?

Bill wagged his head as he cautiously entered the clearing. He looked around, but as usual he was the first to arrive. *Always me*, he groaned, sucking his top lip into his mouth in an effort to clear a swath of swamp grass jammed between two molars. The grass wouldn't budge. *It figures, now when everybody shows up I can grin at them with strings of green hanging from my mouth. How picturesque.* He wagged his head again and stopped in the middle of the glade.

It was an annual thing, this gathering of bull moose in a secluded clearing 127 furlongs northeast of The Pas, Manitoba. Leave it to tradition to pick a place swarming with black flies, mosquitoes, tiger flies and other assorted meat-eating gnats. Of course no one in their right minds would ever come to such a place by choice. Except bull moose, that is. After all, secrecy was paramount.

For hundreds, maybe thousands of years, observers of moose had been the victims of the ultimate deception, an example of sleight-of-hoof trickery unparalleled in the animal kingdom.

Picture the standard shot of a bull moose, the kind seen on nature shows and in calendars found in tourist shops full of shelves cluttered with knickknacks and gewgaws. Standing in some smelly pond, swamp grass hanging from mouth. On its head there'd be a gorgeous, moss-be-decked rack. A palmate rack spanning, what, five feet, furred brown and green with the tips of the tines all polished smooth. Maybe in Alaska, or Quebec, or anywhere in between, wherever there's boreal forest and scuzzy swamps. And below the picture a caption reading *Bull Moose Feeding, Alces americana* when it should be reading *Bull Moose Posing, antlers fakirama.*

There was, in fact, only one rack, one real set of palmate antlers made of genuine organically grown moose hair, and it was a beauty. The set seen in the standard picture in the calendars was a cheap imitation, a plastic replica artfully glued to the moose's head.

Bill realized his ears were twitching. A nervous tick had probably burrowed into his brain and was pushing knobs and pulling switches. *Just my luck. Where are the others, anyway? I'm always first.*

That, of course, was as it should be. For the sixth year running, Bill was the designated Runner. He'd be given the rack in a solemn ritual, passed from the Big Cheese's head (last year's winner) to his own. But would he get to keep it? No way. Hide and seek. They'd give him an hour, then they'd be on his trail, a free-for-all moose hunt. And whoever caught him first would get the rack, for a whole year.

Why am I always "it?" It's not fair. Bill kicked at a tuft of moss. *Who decides these things, anyway?*

Well. Bill's eyes narrowed. He looked around suspiciously, but he was still alone. Good. An idea had come to him, bursting into his rather elongated brain like a smallmouth bass hiding in a mouthful of swamp grass and trying to swim up through the top of his thick skull. He winced in recollection and ducked his head. But Gods, what an idea!

Bill grinned a green, weedy grin. This year it would be different. No more trying to hide behind trees, or crouching behind rotting stumps and sneezing mushroom pollen. Never again would he try to climb a cliff, or bury himself in muskeg with two straws stuck in his nostrils. No more swallowing big rocks and jumping into a deep lake.

Bill snorted angrily. Not this time, he vowed. And never again. This time—*this time*—once he got the rack on his head, it wasn't going to come off. Ever. "They'll not catch me," he whispered. "They won't even find me." He looked down to check his legs. Still four in number. Satisfied, Bill danced around the glade, kicking his hoofs high into the air and flinging mucky things in every direction.

*

Karen crouched in the woods beside the old state highway, the humped hills of western Kentucky rising on all sides. It was just a few minutes past dawn, and she could feel her tiny heart rapping away in her chest. She scampered in circles a few times to burn off some of the nervous excitement, then turned once again to the travelling wardrobe hanging from a hook on a low branch. She reached up and unzipped it.

What would she be this morning? she wondered. Raccoon? Skunk? Antelope? Maybe a cougar—no, she was a cougar just a few days ago. Nose twitching in agitation, Karen rummaged through the wardrobe. Ah! Here was one she hadn't been in ages! With many grunts and frantic pulling she removed the suit.

She was going all the way this morning. Change of scenery was in order. Too easy to end up in a soup pot in this state. And what all that meant was—Karen unzipped the front of the mangy suit—*grille surfing*!

Good thing us possums are insectivores, she decided as she clambered into the foul-smelling fur bag. Just open the mouth and let it happen. The suit's arms were much longer than her own, which was perfect—they dangled like every bone in them was busted up. And there was enough belly room to hold her travelling wardrobe once folded a few times. Made walking a little tricky, but what the hell, she wasn't going far.

By stretching her neck and bunching up the body under her armpits, Karen managed to push her head into the suit's head and look out through the glass eyes. Her own long-jawed mouth fitted snugly into the suit's mouth. She snorted to clear her nose of mange dust, then waddled to the edge of the woods.

The highway beckoned, no traffic in sight. By the time Karen reached the gravel shoulder she was gasping. This would be a hot one, at least at first. She eyed the shoulder, studying tire tracks. The key to playing roadkill lay in how close she could get to those tires whizzing past without getting squished flat. The sheer thrill of it all!

But today she wasn't going to just lie there chuckling to herself with every car passing by, sneering unseen at the open-mouthed pasty faces staring at her from behind tinted windows. She'd warm up that way, sure, but when the time was right, when she'd picked her target churning down the road at sixty miles an hour, she'd make her move.

Grille surfing's tricky business. The ultimate in kicks. Few possums had the guts to even try. Karen knew she was the best, knew she was a goddamn legend.

She took her position on the gravel shoulder, then flopped down, limbs akimbo and head thrown back, tongue dangling. Man, she thought, eyes are gonna pop right out of their sockets.

The hardest part about grille surfing, of course, had to do with the initial launch phase. It had to be finessed perfectly. One mistake and she'd be through the radiator like Edam through a steel sieve. You either had it or you didn't.

Karen had it. And moments after taking position on the road's shoulder she heard the roar of a semitrailer truck coming up from the south, and she knew that here was her ticket to heaven. No warmups after all. A possum afraid to take the big risks might as well curl up and die. The ground shook with the approaching giant. She heard it gear down. The driver wanted a look-see at Mrs Roadkill—even better. She pictured the guy's ogling face, his shoulders hunched in stunned amazement, one leg jumping all over the clutch. *Fantastic!*

Karen tensed as the massive machine thundered up doing an even fifty miles an hour, and at the perfect moment, she hit launch sequence. Flinging herself into the semi's path she caught a brief glimpse of glittering grille filling her world, then *wham!* Shoulder roll and high G plastering her, face outward, onto the bug-spattered screen, arms and legs spread wide.

Karen loosed a wild wind-whipped laugh. Glorious! A grasshopper slammed into the roof of her mouth with a meaty crunch and she reflexively swallowed. Yum, delicious. She licked her lips, then cranked open her mouth once again and squeezed shut her streaming eyes.

*

Crusty Jim sat behind the wheel of his brand new orange Volkswagon van and hummed a contented tune. He'd just come down from Manistikwan Lake, near Flin Flon, after three weeks of fishing. In the back of the van stood a propane-powered freezer crammed full of northern pike, not one under ten pounds. And this year, Crusty Jim had bagged a thirty-eight pounder. A beauty.

He slowed the van down and squinted. Up ahead a moose lay in the middle of the highway, its four legs sticking up into the air. Jim wagged his head. Most of the time when a car or truck hit a moose, the animal would just up and run away, leaving behind a totalled vehicle. He slowed down some more, frowning. Strange. Checking his mirrors he saw that he was alone—no other cars in sight. He stopped the van in front of the beast and set the brake.

"Freeze," a heavy voice growled beside him. Crusty Jim jumped in his seat and turned to his side window to find himself staring into the wide, pulsing nostrils of a second moose. "Put your hands on your head, buster."

The one on the road clambered to its feet, grinning. Two other bulls emerged from the forest edge and hurried up to the van. One looked into the back. "Not much room in there, Jocko," this one said. "There's a freezer bolted to the floor."

"What is all this?" Crusty Jim demanded, his hands still on his head and his eyes rolling from one hairy brown ungulate to the next. Funny, three of them wore plastic antlers, but the biggest, meanest-looking one—the one who had spoken first and was called Jocko—was bare headed.

Jocko's hot, weedy breath gusted into Crusty Jim's face as the moose laughed nastily. "It's a hijack, buster. We're stealing your van."

Crusty Jim narrowed his eyes. He thought furiously. "Any of you guys got a driver's license?"

Jocko's brows knitted. His right ear twitched. "Hey Evander," he called to the moose who'd been lying on the road. The animal ambled up. "You got a license, don't ya?"

Evander shook his broad head. "I'll be of age next year, Jocko," he said.

Crusty Jim stared at the moose. "Your name is Evander?" he asked incredulously.

"Evander Reedfellow," the moose replied loftily. "This entire plan was my idea," he said. "I'm a genius of no modest proportion, mister— mister?"

"Jim. First name's Crusty. Listen," he said, "you don't need to steal my van. I'll do the driving, if it's not too far out of the way."

"There's no telling, Mister Jim," Evander said. "We are on the trail of a diabolical truant. The young lad already has quite a lead on us."

"Enough talk!" Jocko growled, glaring up and down the highway.

"Bally, you climb on top. Evander, you, me, and Beanpole Joe—inside."

The van rocked back and forth and the shocks groaned as the bulls clambered aboard. Crusty Jim stared at the moose folded up in the passenger seat, knees jammed against the roof. Beanpole Joe studied the highway ahead, steadily chewing a mouthful of cud. Crusty Jim continued staring. After a moment Beanpole Joe paused in his chewing, suddenly uneasy.

Crusty Jim spoke carefully. "Did you know that you have a windshield wiper sticking out of your left ear?"

Beanpole Joe blinked at the man. "That's okay."

"It is?"

The moose nodded sagely. "It doesn't work anymore."

"Oh, I see." Crusty cleared his throat. "And the sideview mirror in your right nostril, is it also broken?"

Beanpole Joe frowned. "What mirror?"

Evander Reedfellow's head came in between them. "If you will start driving, I can explain," he said, jerking his head at Beanpole Joe and rolling his eyes.

"Right." Crusty Jim started the van rolling. "Which way?"

"South. The way you're going, fortunately."

Crusty Jim risked a glance into the back of the van. "Can't figure out how all you guys fit in there."

"Yes, it is cramped." Evander studied the ceiling, as if preparing for a lecture. "As you may know, Mister Jim, each year there are hundreds of incidents involving head-on collisions between moose and vehicles. What may well astonish you is that Beanpole Joe here is responsible for all of them. Whether in the Yukon or in Minnesota, there is but one moose waging perpetual war against cars and trucks."

"I hit a train once," Beanpole Joe said, his glassy gaze fixed on the highway beyond the windshield.

Crusty Jim waited. "And?"

"It hurt."

"Can't this damn thing go any faster?" Jocko demanded.

"We're overloaded," Crusty Jim said. "Besides, we're doing fifty right now. This truant you're after can run that fast, can he?"

"Of course not," Evander said. "As I mentioned earlier, however, Bill has quite a start on us."

"Oh, like how far?"

"We have it on good authority that he is somewhere east of Minneapolis."

"What?" Crusty Jim started braking. "No way in hell I'm going—"

"Drive!" Jocko roared in the man's ear.

"All right, all right," Jim said, wincing. "But when we get to the border, Evander, you do the talking."

"Of course," Evander said.

*

Tank Sergeant Merv Redflag, the muscles of his heavy jaw bouncing around as he gritted his teeth, scanned the hills through his field glasses. He sighed. Getting separated from his platoon was one thing, but he had a growing suspicion that he wasn't even in Nebraska anymore.

He looked down on his driver, Jiggs. The man had his Walkman on and was flipping through a comic book. Merv stretched a leg down and kicked Jiggs in the head. Jiggs looked up.

"You got a radio station on there, Jiggs?" Merv growled.

"Yup. Des Moines. The news just came on. Seems there's a moose running across Iowa, Sarge."

Tank Sergeant Merv Redflag's eyes lit up. "The hell with the war games, son. Load up the main armament." He scanned the hills again, grinding his teeth.

"We in Iowa, Sarge?"

"Just roll east, son, roll east. We're gonna bag us a moose, hah."

Down below, Jiggs glanced over at Toes, the gunner. "Iowa's a big state, ain't it, Toes?"

Toes shrugged. "We got a government issue Conoco credit card, right? Sarge says roll, we roll."

"You loaded?" Jiggs asked.

Toes grinned around his grape-flavoured Hubba Bubba. "Steel-jacketed armour-piercing mayhem. Laser-tracking digital array. And like our motto goes, 'If you see it, kill it.' "

Jiggs frowned as he activated the gyrostabilizer. "That our motto?"
Toes smacked his gum. "Something like that, anyway."

*

Crusty Jim checked his watch. It read three a.m. He pried one hand from
the steering wheel and rubbed his eyes. Up ahead rose the glow of the
border station. He slowed down. "All right, US Customs dead ahead.
You ready for this, Evander?"

The moose nodded confidently. "There is no need to worry, Mister
Jim."

The fisherman grunted. They rolled up to the first booth inside which
waited a Customs officer. The man held up a hand and Crusty Jim braked
and lowered the window. He stopped the van opposite the booth and the
officer stepped outside.

"Good evening," he said, leaning over for a look-see. He raised a
flashlight and flicked it on just as Beanpole Joe turned to stare at him.
The beam flashed off the mirror in Beanpole Joe's nostril. "Yikes!" the
officer yelped, stepping back and squeezing shut his eyes. He took a moment to regain his composure than leaned back down. Tears streaming
from his eyes, he asked, "Are you transporting any vegetable matter?"

"None undigested, sir," Evander said.

"Uh huh. Any livestock?"

"Hardly," Crusty Jim replied.

"Hmm hmm.What about this moose on your roof?"

"I'm not dead," Bally muttered. "Though my lips have peeled back
and stayed that way and I haven't blinked in hours."

"Oh," the officer said, frowning.

"Sir?" Evander leaned forward. "We have nothing to declare. Nothing at all."

"Very good," the officer said. "I suppose moose don't really qualify
as livestock, do they? Welcome to the United States." He smiled and
straightened, and waved a hand. "Drive on."

Crusty Jim complied. Once out of the light he shook his head. *Yanks.*

"I have an arrest record," Beanpole Joe said. "I'm glad he didn't
ask."

"And I'm equally glad you didn't offer that tidbit of information," Evander said, rolling his eyes.

"I thought about it," Beanpole Joe said.

Crusty Jim waited for the moose to continue. He didn't. The fisherman pushed his arms against the steering wheel until his joints cracked. "I hate to say this, guys, but I'm beat. I could use a cup of coffee."

Evander nodded. "Yes. Furthermore, it is pee-pee time and perhaps even poo-poo time for us. May I suggest we stop at the next truckstop."

Crusty Jim, whose hair was sopping from Jocko's gusty snores, floored the gas pedal in anticipation, his bloodshot eyes straining for the next pool of light on the side of the highway.

*

Karen groaned. Four states nonstop, not to mention that disastrous decision just outside of Des Moines. She saw the cloud up ahead, knew what it was, but she kept her mouth open anyway. Karen groaned again, massaging her distended stomach. "I swear," she whispered, "not one more locust. Not ever!" Thousands of the damn things, and piled on top of bumble bees, wasps, dragonflies, gnats and one scatterbrained crow, she was as close to exploding as a possum could get.

"This one's for the record books," she said, trying to console the misery of her situation with visions of the legends in the making. A four-state grille surf, nonstop, two and a half days. Incredible. Mind-blowing.

Blearily she looked up. They'd finally stopped.

Beyond the light of the roadside cafe rolled flatlands under a crystal clear midnight sky. She tried moving an arm, failed. Gads, it was agony. Better just stay where I am for a while, let the blood start flowing again. Amazing!

*

Jocko and his three allies stood outside the van watching Crusty Jim struggle his way into a lone pushup on the parking lot's oil-stained gravel.

Sheer futility. Jocko drew a deep breath and glared about. He scowled

41

at Bally Payne. "Wipe that damn grin off your face. You look like an idiot."

"I can't," Bally said.

Jocko swung his attention to the cafe's front door. "Well, let's head inside." He led the way between the parked semitrailers. After a moment Crusty Jim gave up on the pushup and clambered to his feet. Wiping the sweat from his brow, he followed the bulls into the cafe.

The four moose burst into the restaurant, shouldering people out of the way and stamping up to the counter. "Where's the bathroom?" Jocko demanded of the waitress.

The girl blanched, then pointed.

"Canadians," someone whispered at one of the tables. "Funny," another replied. "They don't look French."

The moose hurried into the bathroom and slammed the door. Crusty Jim took a seat at the counter. "Some coffee please," he said to the waitress.

"M-mm-me t-t-too," a trucker beside him stuttered.

Crusty Jim studied the man. He looked like hell. The guy shook like a bowl of jello. Deep black rings encircled bugged-out, chicken-embryo eyes. His hair stood on end, frizzy as if zapped a thousand times by lightning. "Pretty jittery there," Crusty Jim said. "Something wrong?"

The trucker's bulging eyes remained staring straight ahead. "T-t-that's m-m-mmy rig out th-th-there. Th-th-the f-f-f-f irst one."

Crusty Jim looked. "You mean the one with the polar bear clinging to the grille?"

The trucker nodded. Tears welled in his eyes and he suddenly spun and clutched the front of Crusty's shirt. He pushed his face into the fisherman's and snarled, "I had to stop! Don't you see! I had to! I couldn't go on—I tried, my God I tried! Polar bears in Kentucky! I just kept going, you understand? Kept going!" His head whipped around as the front door opened. "Aaagh! It's come for me! Aaagh!" The trucker let go of Crusty's shirt and leapt over the counter, landing at the waitress's feet with a heavy thump.

Crusty Jim stared at the weird beast standing in the doorway. After a moment the fisherman scowled. "You're no polar bear," he said.

Karen peeked out through the bear's gaping, bug-spattered mouth. "Not so loud!" she hissed, ambling up to the man. A short hop brought her up onto the stool just vacated by the trucker, who was busy climbing into an automatic dishwasher in the kitchen. "Buy me a beer, will you?" Karen flopped her bear arms down on the counter.

"What kind of animal are you?"

Karen shrugged. "Possum, what else? What about that beer?"

"A beer for the bear, waitress."

"What state is this?" Karen asked.

"Minnesota," Crusty Jim answered.

"Yikes, that's way out of my natural habitat. I gotta head back south. Which way you going, bud?" The beer arrived and the possum closed her massive paws around the bottle.

Crusty Jim slowly shut his eyes. "South. But it'd be a crowded trip. I'm warning you now."

"The name's Karen." The possum swallowed a mouthful of beer and sighed gustily. "I don't mind the cramp," she said. "So long as I don't have to ride another grille."

The bathroom door slammed open and the four moose piled out, looking around guiltily. Moving in a tight clump, they headed for the door. As he passed Crusty, Evander whispered, "We'll be in the van. Bally had an accident."

The fisherman scowled at the grinning culprit, then pulled out his wallet. "Drink up," he told Karen. "We're getting out of here."

*

Tank Sergeant Merv Redflag adjusted the range on his field glasses. "All right," he growled. "There's a blob of heat coming up fast over that hill in front of us. It's got antlers. Initiate laser sighting, get us a fix on the baby, Toes. Let's blast it out of existence, hah."

Below him Jiggs pushed himself forward in his seat and pressed his face against the bow port. "Hey Sarge," he said. "Antlers? I think—"

"Target acquisition confirmed!" Toes shouted.

"Tracking locked on!"

"Sarge?" Jiggs said. "That heat blob—"

"Fire!" Merv bellowed.

The tank rocked. On the hill Jiggs saw a puff of smoke bloom where the tractor had been. A moment later a farmer wobbled out from the white and brown cloud.

"Target hit, hah!" Merv thumped the turret. "Good shooting, Toes! Hot damn!"

Jiggs studied the map on his knees. "Sarge? That hill's in Kansas. We just shot across a state line." He looked at Toes. "Can we do that?"

Toes shrugged. "Beats me."

"We fried a tractor," Jiggs said, glancing out the window again. "That farmer's coming up on us fast. He looks real mad."

"Incoming missile!" Merv shrieked. "Evasive maneuvers!"

Jiggs hit the throttle. The tank surged forward.

"Whatcha doing?" Toes asked.

"Going straight at the guy," Jiggs said, leaning forward. "I won't run him down, not really." He licked his lips as the bouncing tank picked up speed.

"He running yet?" Toes wanted to know.

"Uh, straight at us." Jiggs frowned. "Looks like he's got a shotgun."

"You don't think he'd use it, do you?" Toes was sweating.

"Sure as hell hope not," Jiggs said. "You know what a shotgun could do to all these sensitive computers and stuff?"

Toes shivered. "Don't I know it, bud, don't I know it."

Merv screamed, "Get us out of here, Jiggs!"

Jiggs spun the wheel, throwing everyone to one side. "All right," he growled. "Warp Drive, here we go!"

*

"Damn tires are wearing out," Crusty Jim complained, giving one of them the boot.

Jocko stuck his head out a window. "Lose the bear and let's get going," he said.

Crusty Jim frowned. "Where's Bally," he asked, looking at the empty roof.

"He's in here," Evander said. "We've decided to increase the molecular density of this vehicle, in case there's trouble."

"What? What kind of trouble?"

"There's no telling, Mister Jim."

Crusty Jim grunted. "We're giving the bear a ride, so make room."

Everyone groaned as Karen climbed in. "I'm not really a bear," she explained. "I'm a possum."

"You appear too fat to be a possum," Evander said.

"Shut up," she snapped.

Behind the wheel, Crusty Jim paused before starting the engine. "So what about my tires?" he demanded.

"They will not be a problem, Mister Jim," Evander said. "I have anticipated this difficulty and have come up with a plan."

"I smell fish," Karen said, wiggling her nose in the cab's musty air. "Northern pike, I think. Equis lummox."

"Yes," Evander said. "We have removed the freezer."

"You what?" Crusty Jim screamed.

"It's all right," Evander said. "The frozen fish remain with us, packed here and there around our bodies. I believe they will not thaw for approximately eighteen and one half hours, and until then they make good clublike weapons, if necessary."

"I've got a salmon suit," Karen said.

"Let's move!" Jocko roared.

*

It was an hour before dawn. Inches from the ceiling lamp, Karen squirmed and grunted, trying to get comfortable. She had her Walkman on, running through radio stations. They'd just crossed another state line. She hit a station in Kansas and caught a word that made her stiffen. Eyes narrowing, she listened carefully for a few minutes, then snatched off her headphones.

"Trouble, guys," she said. "Your buddy Bill was spotted in a disco bar just on the outskirts of Kansas City. The police were called in, but the moose made a successful getaway, stealing a semitrailer. He's somewhere on the interstate heading south. I didn't know he knew how to drive."

"He can't," Evander said. His eyes widened and he whispered, "My God."

Karen stared at the moose for a moment, then said, "Well. There's more. Some tank that was supposed to be in a war-game exercise in Nebraska is in hot pursuit of your friend."

"My God," Evander whispered again. "Hunters."

Crusty Jim swore. "So I guess your friend Bill's about to become minced moosemeat, huh."

Evander slowly shook his head. "You don't understand. Bill has the Rack. It has, uh, special powers."

Karen continued staring at Evander. "Anyway," she said, "there's road blocks ahead."

Crusty Jim ground his teeth until he felt grit in his mouth. "So what do we do now, eh? Come on, Mister Brainiac, I'm waiting."

"We must simply run through the roadblocks," the moose said. "The US Army and the Highway Patrol will not be able to stop Bill. And as for us, our innate density should be sufficient to carry us through."

"No kidding," Karen muttered.

*

Toes stuffed three more Hubba Bubbas into his mouth. The air in the tank reeked of Conoco Number 3.

Jiggs, hunched down over the wheel, pulled off his headphones and threw Toes a wild look. "Some orange Volkswagon van's on our trail. Blasted through a roadblock like it wasn't even there."

"Damn," Toes said. "More hunters. We could end up in a free-for-all . . . against genuine American citizens armed with guns and spears and stuff . . ."

Jiggs's eyes went wide. "And all's we got is this damned tank. We won't stand a chance!"

*

"What did I tell you," Evander said. "Not a scratch, not a dent."

Crusty Jim pried a bloodless hand from the steering wheel and rubbed his neck. "We're in a whole lot of trouble, guys ."

46

"Just keep driving," Jocko said.

"Listen," Crusty Jim snapped. "The shocks have had it and those tires gotta be ready to blow any second, and then what?"

Evander sighed. "Very well, Mister Jim. Stop the vehicle. We will initiate my backup plan."

Crusty Jim eased the van onto the shoulder and rolled it to a stop. "Heading out to stretch my legs," he said.

"Very well," Evander said.

Crusty Jim climbed out and walked down into the ditch. He unzipped his pants. Behind him he heard dreadful crunching sounds, and winced. Whatever they were up to, it sounded bad. Finished with his watering he closed up the zipper and turned around. "Oh no," he moaned.

Evander stuck his head out the side window. "We're ready."

The van's four wheels dangled a foot off the ground, a forest of brown knobby legs sticking out from the undercarriage.

Karen stood beside Crusty Jim, her bear paws on her hips. "These friends of yours, Crusty . . ." She shook her head. "Not all there, if you ask me."

Crusty Jim released an exhausted sigh, said nothing.

"Something strange," Karen said. "Four moose in there, right?"

"Right."

"Then how come I count seventeen legs?"

*

The tank slammed to a stop, throwing Merv Redflag against the rim of the turret hatch. The air whooshed from his lungs and he spent the next few moments frantically scratching at the metal and turning blue in the face.

Jiggs waited down below. "Sarge? Where to now?" Through his viewfinder, a narrow gravel road wound its way through cypress trees.

Merv finally regained his breath. "Stop doing that!"

Jiggs ducked. "Sorry."

Merv strapped on his infrared goggles and studied the map on his lap. He frowned. Everything was gray. "How in hell do they—" He shook his head, no sir, never question Uncle Sam. "We're in Louisiana, Jiggs.

And that's the road we want." He looked up and glared about. "I can smell that damn moose," he hissed. "Toes," he called down. "From now on, everything that moves, kill it."

"Gotcha."

"Move her out," Merv ordered. "Nice and slow."

*

Seventeen legs pumping unceasingly, they made good time. Crusty Jim, his feet up on the dashboard and his hands behind his head, glanced over at a gasping Evander. "Something I've been meaning to ask you guys."

"What?"

"How're you trailing this Bill?"

"Yeah," Karen said. "I've been wondering that, too."

"Well," Evander said, "I'm due for a rest anyway. Just a moment while I pull my legs up."

"Pansy," Jocko sneered, froth gathering at the corners of his mouth.

Evander brought his front knees up and propped his furry chin on them. "You see, us moose have been around for a long time. Way back, before you people arrived, every bull moose had its own rack. Daddy just handed it down to Junior, and so on. But then you people started hunting us and putting those racks, sans heads, up on cave walls, hut walls, tipi walls and cabin walls and restaurant walls. Racks got scarce. Anyway, we finally came up with the annual contest. Problem was, every now and then, one of the designated runners got it into his head to keep the rack. And off he went. So now, of course, there's only one rack left, and Bill has it."

"And," Jocko growled, "it belongs to me!"

"We moose," Evander said, "are a predictable lot. When we run, we run due south, and we don't stop until we find a swamp."

Crusty Jim looked around. "Like, say, Louisiana."

"Correct."

Jocko said, "Get your legs back in action, Reedfellow. It's your turn to run backwards, remember."

Evander groaned and grunted and snorted until his tail faced the windshield.

Karen leaned closed to Crusty. "Let's hope he's not as long-winded on this end, huh?"

*

Merv leaned down and whispered, "Nice and easy, Jiggs, bring her to a full stop." He scanned the surrounding swamp through his infrared goggles. "Perfect. Load up, Toes, I want steel-jacket, armour-piercing main armament up and ready." He sniffed the air. "Stick-legged birds, small furry animals, butterflies, and moose—this place is an American hunter's dream."

*

Ten feet away, El Shoe licked his lips. *I can wait. I can wait a thousand years, a million. I'm ready. I'm always ready. Blink the lids. Pump the tongue. Look inconspicuous. I'm an alligator. Eating things is my job. I can wait a thousand years, and you know why? I'm brainless. That's right, brainless. I'm waiting. I'm still waiting, dammit.*

*

"Hang left!" Jocko roared. The van rocked, heeled sharply, skidding over gravel and raising a cloud of dust, then the churning legs underneath dug in and they surged through the turn.

Crusty Jim and Karen leaned forward, scanning the winding road ahead and the crowding trees on either side.

They picked up speed until the forest raced past in a blur. As they rounded a sharp bend everyone screamed. Immediately in front of them sat an M-1 tank. A helmeted sergeant was visible from the chest up at the turret. He spun around and his jaw dropped as the van bore down on him.

*

From his vantage point El Shoe could see, beyond the tank, the top of the Volkswagon and part of the windshield. The vehicle looked crowded, packed even.

I'm ready, no more waiting. This is it. Grease the hinges. Here it comes. Tourists like so many sardines. Unsuspecting. Got their cameras out. I'm ready. Ready for the big picture. Here it comes. Open wide. No more waiting. Who needs brains. What a life.

*

At the last moment the van's thundering legs pushed right. The van spun a full three hundred and sixty degrees as it swerved around the tank and then was past, picking up speed once again.

They topped the rise at ninety-two miles an hour. Just past it was a shallow depression, which turned out to be real bumpy. But only for a moment, then everything smoothed out again.

"That felt kind of funny," Bally said.

Evander's tail twitched. "I agree. A very odd feeling."

"Felt good," Beanpole Joe said.

*

"After them!" Merv shrieked. "That van was full of moose! And a polar bear! After them!"

Jiggs hit the throttle, and the tank roared forward, into and out of the depression, across a bumpy bit, then away.

*

Oh God. El Shoe opened one bloodshot eye. *I feel wider, longer, flatter. A hundred million years. For what? Turned into an enormous handbag. Where are my brains? Those feet. Big. Whatever happened to tires? And tank treads. Big. I can't win. Got no brains Power of anticipation a weak point in this evolutionary scheme. A hundred million years. For what? I'm still brainless.*

El Shoe blinked. Something pink and fuzzy and hovering approached. He struggled to focus. *Oh God, a pink flamingo. Come to gloat. Ugh, kicking sand in my face. So much for dignity.*

Just give me a minute, Stick-legs. One minute to pull myself together. That's all I need. Then snap! Regurgitating feathers for three days. One minute, that's all. I'm one mean bastard and I've still got big teeth— somewhere around here, hold on, just let me find them . . .

*

Karen eyed the swamp for a moment, paws on hips, then nodded. "All right," she said. "I'll do it."

"Excellent," Evander said. "What will you go as, then?"

"Not sure. Let me check my wardrobe."

Crusty Jim sighed and turned to survey his van. The moose had driven it off the road into some bushes. Having then piled out, they left—to the mystery of everyone—one moose leg still standing. The Volkswagon tottered and leaned on this one leg but refused to fall over. Crusty shook his head in wonderment.

"This'll do," Karen said.

"Ingenious," Evander commented.

Crusty turned. Way up the road stood Beanpole Joe as their rear guard. They figured the tank was still on their trail, probably still a mile or two back. Bally Payne and Jocko waited in the nearby ditch, twitching their ears and tails in frustration. Evander and Karen crouched just at the swamp's edge. The plan was for Karen to enter in disguise and suss things out. The possum had removed from her wardrobe a pink flamingo suit and was explaining its operating procedure to Evander.

"The stick-legs got handles up here inside, see?" Karen opened the suit's round body to display the instruments. "I use my back feet on those, properly strapped in, of course."

"Of course," Evander said.

"And with my front feet I move the neck and head around, like this. "She reached inside and the flamingo's head spun three hundred sixty degrees.

"Remarkable," Evander said.

Beanpole Joe came running back. "There's a dust cloud approaching."

Jocko and Bally joined the group. "All right," Jocko said. "Get into the damn suit, Karen, and let's all get back into the van. Bill's close. I can feel it."

Beanpole Joe fidgeted. "Jocko?" he asked. "Can't I run into the tank?"

"No," Jocko snapped. "Let's move!"

Crusty Jim followed the flamingo and the four moose back to the van. He watched the animals pile in, but no extra legs showed beneath the vehicle. There was some quiet muttering inside the van, then Evander stuck his head out and grinned sheepishly at Crusty Jim.

"What's wrong?"

"Well, Mister Jim. It seems your fish have frozen into a solid mass, somewhat like a carpet. I'm afraid we may have trouble getting our feet through."

From up the road came the roar of the tank.

"Quickly, Mister Jim. We can still get away."

Crusty Jim climbed into the front seat.

*

Merv's eyes streamed as he glared steadily up the road. They came to a rise. "Target sighted!" Merv screamed. "I want acquisition, now!"

Down below, Toes leaned forward and pressed his face against the viewfinder. Up ahead an orange van bounced down the road on one long, brown leg. He activated the laser sights.

"I want acquisition!" Merv shrieked.

"I'm trying!" Toes yelled back. "Jiggs, bring us closer, dammit!"

"That van's moving fast!" Jiggs said, wiping sweat from his brow.

"Locked on, locked on!"

"Fire!" Merv bellowed.

*

Steel-jacketed, armour-piercing shell struck high innate density. A massive explosion ripped the air, thundered the earth, gouted flame and smoke in a mushroom cloud skyward. The echoes of the detonation rolled through the swamp like a shiver of doom.

Deep in the wet shadows, Bill flinched and looked around wildly. *Oh no, they've found me.* This was terrible. And worse, *I've got this terrible urge to stampede. I didn't know us moose liked to stampede. I suppose we rarely get the chance.*

All around him, he heard a soft rustling, distant splashing, a general subsonic surge of movement. He wondered at its source, but he could not resist the call.

Stampede!

As he began moving forward, inexorably, feeling the power surging from the rack and down into his knobby, elongated, hairy body, the sky began to rain fish.

*

The smoke cleared. Tank Sergeant Merv Redflag stared.

Down below, Jiggs and Toes heard their commander whisper: "My god, it's full of roadkill!"

*

"One good thing," Evander said amidst the jumble of legs and broken plastic antlers, "about having a natural habitat characterized by swamp is that should you be blown out of a Volkswagon van by an M-1 tank shell, you inevitably land in soft squishy places."

Crusty Jim wiped muck from his face and sat up blearily. He watched a bedraggled pink flamingo stagger out from the bushes and approach the crater where the van had been.

"Fantastic" Karen said.

Her travelling wardrobe had exploded. Animals suits lay everywhere, like some kind of roadkill graveyard. Snow leopard, hippo, gemsbock, walrus, gibbon, lemur, ground sloth, tapir, salmon, alligator—hundreds of crumpled animals, flung about and motionless, cast out to all sides.

"Incredible!" Karen whispered, stepping into the midst of the scene. She had no idea she had so many. They looked so real, especially that alligator . . .

Frowning, Karen jiggled the toggle switch, moving her suit forward for a closer look. Talk about realistic. She leaned down for a closer look.

*

So much for waiting. Vengeance at last. What's a hundred million years, after all. Come closer, little bird. Come closer.

*

Crusty Jim stood up and staggered into the clearing. A dull rumbling sound filled the air, getting louder. He glanced in the direction of the swamp, saw nothing. Unaccountably uneasy, Crusty Jim looked around.

He saw Karen approach an alligator, the bird head dipping down for a closer look. A sudden explosion of feathers and a loud squawk, and from somewhere inside the alligator's mouth came Karen's frantic scream: "Eject! Eject!"

*

Merv's eyes bugged out as he watched the flamingo burst from the alligator's mouth in a gout of flame. Something small and furry flew out from the cloud of pink feathers—directly toward Merv.

"Incoming! Incoming!"

Down below, Jiggs looked at Toes. Toes looked at Jiggs. There was a soft thump, then nothing.

Toes cocked his head. "You hear rumbling sounds, Jiggs?"

"Maybe," Jiggs said. "Hey Sarge?"

No answer. Toes moved slightly and glanced up. "He's gone." He sat back down, suddenly nervous. "I'm loading another shell, Jiggs. I've got a bad feeling about this."

"Go up for a look first," Jiggs said.

"No, Jiggs, you're up."

Groaning, Jiggs climbed up the stepladder. Once clear of the turret hatch, he looked around. Feathers floated in the air. Tank Sergeant Merv was running down the road as fast as his small legs could carry him. Jiggs frowned, then he heard screaming and turned.

*

Crusty Jim's jaw dropped. He had no time to even think about Karen's glorious demise. From out of the swamp's forest came a sea of movement, brown humped shoulders, enormous racks, thundering legs, and among them, a thirty-eight-pound pike with a single leg sticking out of its mouth.

"Stampede!" Evander screamed. "We're doomed!"

The four bull moose cowered in a tight clump, directly in the stampeding path of thousands, and thousands, of rack-bearing runners. In the lead ran Bill, closely followed by the northern pike.

Crusty scrambled and dove headfirst behind Jocko, Evander, Bally

Payne and a grinning Beanpole Joe.

*

Jiggs dropped back down into the chassis compartment, his face white as he stared at Toes.

"Fire," he said.

Toes had unbreached the main gun and was staring down the barrel length. "I can't. The barrel's jammed."

"Fire," Jiggs said.

"There's something in the barrel."

"Close the breach and fire," Jiggs said.

Toes closed the breach and looked at Jiggs. "Something all furry—"

"FIRE!" Jiggs screamed.

Toes fired.

*

Karen's eyes streamed tears. She caught a momentary vision of a thousand-antlered moose in front of her, a rushing wall that magically parted around her. Then it was gone, and blue sky beckoned ahead.

"Fantastic!"

She barely had time to open her mouth before hitting the flock of pelicans that had been winging northward but were now wheeling about catching frozen fish high above the swamp.

*

"You've done it!" Jiggs yelled. "It parted! It parted like the Brown Sea!"

"Red Sea, you mean," Toes said, loading his mouth with more Hubba Bubba.

"No," Jiggs said firmly. "It was brown."

"I wish it wasn't so dark in here," Toes said. "I've got this eerie feeling."

Jiggs crouched low, sighing, then he frowned, looking down. "The floor's all lumpy, Toes." He reached down and probed with his fingertips. "Pebbly, slick, slightly cool. Hey, you're not wearing alligator shoes, are you?"

Toes paused in the midst of blowing a large bubble. He looked at Jiggs. "No."

Jiggs looked at Toes.

Toes looked at Jiggs.

*

Crusty Jim slowly climbed to his feet. The dust cloud of the stampede was dwindling to the north.

Jocko and Evander and Bally Payne and Beanpole Joe regained their feet and seemed busy counting hoofs. Then Evander strode over to Crusty Jim. "We're terribly sorry about your van, Mister Jim."

"Forget the van!" Jocko snarled. "They're heading north. Let's get after them!"

Their attention was drawn by a commotion in the tank. It was rocking wildly back and forth. Then it stopped.

Jocko's eyes narrowed. "Hah, that's our ticket."

Crusty Jim stared at the bull. "You must be kidding!"

"Of course," Evander said. "No doubt we'll find a government issue Conoco credit card inside. This, Mister Jim, is ideal."

"All the way back to Manitoba, right?" Crusty Jim sighed. "Okay, but I'm driving."

"Certainly," Evander said. "But allow us to get inside first."

"Sure."

*

El Shoe ran his thick soft tongue over his jagged teeth. Yum. *Three, four days of slow, luxurious digestion. Ahhh, who needs brains? And best of all, here I am, safe from sharp, thumping, agonizing hoofs. Safe, safe for a hundred million years.*

It was then that he heard the turret hatch clang open.

Factory at Capashin

PEOPLE TRY to take him apart all the time. But they can't. In Capashin they say there's only one way to see his face. Build a rocket, get inside, fire it up. And when the prairie down below is the size of a dinner plate, leftovers begging surreal analysis, his face becomes visible. More or less. An eye here, another over there, by the hill, and there's his grimace and French moustache, his Scottish whiskers, his Nordic nose, Ukrainian ears, Ojibwa eyelashes: poor wise-man gaze following the knife in the sky—being the rocket with fattened lips and nose pressed to the porthole.

In Capashin they say there's only one way to see his face. And only one way to hear him. Pick a bitter cold early Spring day and go down on knees, press face to the stubble. And his silence makes sense. He might tell a true story. He might tell a lie. He might say this:

This is the Owner:

He can see his breath, once every fifteen minutes. A wet sheen of white begins to cloud the windshield. He raises a rawhide-gloved hand and turns on the defroster. And then, in the uncertain world beyond the glass, something begins to happen.

And these are the Tricksters:

Five mud-spattered pickup trucks crawl over the hill, fan out from the road, bounce across the open prairie. They circle the hill, then climb to its summit. They stop. Doors open. Bundled men pile out. Dance to fend off the bitter wind. Wave arms to fend off other things.

The Owner:

Grimaces, shuts off the radio that wasn't on, cutting in half a song that wasn't playing, nudges the gas pedal down a fraction of an inch, leans forward on the steering wheel.

The Tricksters:

Reach a concensus that sends them scattering back to their trucks. In moments they are gone, leaving the hill as empty as it had been before. Even though it's not an empty hill in truth. There's a factory on it. Unless, of course, the factory is a lie.

The Owner:

Barks a laugh, grinds his engineless truck into gear, pulls onto the road which, if the factory is a lie, is also a lie, since it's a common belief that roads lead from one place to another, or back again if the other place wasn't worth visiting in the first place.

But on the other hand:

The factory went up in 1934. The CNR laid tracks to service it. Clumps of grain silos were suddenly discovered near the tracks and the CNR station house sometime around 1944. People appeared, brought houses with them, put them up. Then they waited to be offered jobs in the factory. Day after day, year after year, they sat on the porch in front of Gunrod's Cafe, drank coffee and stared at the belching smokestacks on the hill.

After some time, the people found other things to do. They stopped waiting for the factory to open its doors. They came to consider it and its smokestacks as simply another piece of the land. The CNR eventually forgot about the factory, too, and amused itself filling cars with wheat: Volkswagons and triticale in the raccoon coat days, Fargos and barley later.

From 1934 until 1947 the factory belched smoke. No supplies went in. No supplies went out. No one entered it. No one left it.

With one exception. There was the factory owner, whose name was never known, who never spoke with anyone, who never ate, who built a rocket and blasted off into space, who came back down again, who kept a spare eye in his shirt pocket and placed it in the middle of his forehead looking inward, who drove down main street five times a year in his black limousine which had been converted to a pickup truck rear of the front wheels and was a 1934 model with shiny brass grille and deep-dish solid wheels and no engine.

From 1947 until 1997 the factory belched smoke.

The man became known as the Owner. He never spoke. He breathed once every fifteen minutes. He blinked once every five hours. He wore rawhide gloves. He always drove in reverse reverse in drove always he. He had three eyes. He had one nose. He hibernated in winter. He was hiding out from the law. He was the law. He was the Devil. He was God. He wore black coats. He was immortal, immoral, upright, downwrong, wise, stupid, omniscient, a liberal, a priest a professor a woman a Russian spy.

He never spoke. He breathed once . . .

The town became known as Capashin. Said to be a Cree word, its meaning was the subject of occasional discourse. Some said it meant *industry* and pointed fingers at the factory. Others were more direct and insisted the word meant *factory* and pointed fingers at the sky over their heads.

No one asked a Cree. There weren't any around.

Which was not quite the truth. Twenty-two miles to the north, on the far side of the Saskatchewan River, lived a band of Swampy Cree. Originally from the boreal forests of Manitoba, the band was brought by train to their new reserve in 1915.

If asked, the Cree replied that the word *Capashin* was not Cree, but Blackfoot. The Blackfoot, if pursued to Alberta, explained that the word was in fact of English origin and that it meant *factory* (and they would point their fingers down at the earth).

In 1997 the population of Capashin was 357. Down two from the census of 1976. Nobody knew where the two people had gone, and a town meeting was called, to no avail. The two had simply disappeared. Maybe, some whispered, into the factory.

In Capashin, anything was possible even though nothing ever happened. The world changed, however, on June 1, 1997.

A band of Cree arrived in five pickup trucks. They had, they told the town officials, walked to Ottawa and returned in five pickup trucks. They presented a petition claiming all of Saskatchewan and Manitoba as their birthright. But, they reassured the flustered town officials, they would settle for that hill over there.

An agreement was drafted, signed by everyone including four-year-old Billy Reefenshtal, who marked the document with a large X employing Hershey's chocolate as a medium of consent.

The Cree drove away. The meeting was formally closed.

Everyone went home, except for Miss Minutes, who had to take the minutes and record them officially on a typewriter using white-out when necessary; and for the Mayor, who had to go into his office for some reason or other.

People try to take him apart all the time. But they can't. People try to rush him. But they can't. People explain to him the rules, tell him they're there for a reason but never mind the reason because rules are rules.

But in Capashin, people know he takes his time. He might tell a true story. He might tell a lie. He might mislead. He might begin with a prologue, a preamble, a postamble, an epilogue, a critique, a list of household goods.

Or he might jump in his rocket and take off for the skies. He might.

People try to take him apart all the time.

He might jump into a rocket and . . .

MINUTES TO THE CAPASHIN TOWN MEETING, JUNE 1, 1997

12:35 PM. Doors fly open and pickup trucks numbered
           five enter council chambers.
12:41 PM. Chief Negotiator presents petition
           suggests as compromise "that hill over there " (points)
12:59 PM. Agreement signed by Chief Negotiator and
           His Lordship Mayor Preen.

Miss Minutes pauses at her typewriter, glances around her tiny office, gaze fixing on the calendar donated by Hogg Feeds Inc, then on the window overlooking most of the town. She frowns, rises and slowly walks to the window. *Which hill?* she wonders. In her mind's eye, which is capable of recreating scenes in exacting detail of events reaching as far back as last week, Miss Minutes recalls Chief Negotiator standing right about there, near that, his finger pointing out the window, at that angle, which would coincide with (taking into account diurnal ascension and convergent degrees), which would coincide with . . .

Miss Minutes looks out the window. She gasps. Her eyes widen. Her hair stands on end and is permanently turned white. She staggers back. She clutches her breasts. Her mouth drops open. Her uppers clatter to the floor and are kicked under the desk where there's a drain hole, into which they plunge travelling many miles through pipelines to reappear at the beer bottling plant a hundred miles east of Capashin, the bottle passing inspection then being sold and shipped out on a truck for delivery: delivered, removed from the case, served up, contents realized, bottle broken open, uppers returned to Miss Minutes at the next table, there to reside forever more firmly glued to her mastoid process.

Miss Minutes is looking out the window. Her eyes are wide, and her hair is white, and vertical. She is gasping and clutching her breasts, one to each hand.

In the next office Mayor Preen stares into his mirror, deftly removing nose hairs and surgically implanting them into his thinning hairline. The operation is meeting with dubious excess and he softly curses the town of Capashin as a technological backwater.

He pauses, hearing strange noises behind him. He whirls in his chair which he has had especially made so it can go round and round and round and never unscrew. His eyes narrow at the door to Miss Minutes's office, beyond which the sounds are issuing. He rises, walks to the door, opens it, looks inside.

Miss Minutes is looking out the window, kneading her breasts.

Curious, Mayor Preen enters, walks over to the window. "What are you looking at, Miss Minutes?" he asks softly.

In a vacant tone she replies, "The hill."

Mayor Preen raises eyebrows which he has plucked clean long ago. "The hill, you say?" He squints out at it. "What's it got that I don't have, I wonder?"

"That's the hill," Miss Minutes whispers.

"Why yes, so it is."

"The hill the Cree now own."

"What? Really? But that hill's got the—"

Mayor Preen gasps. His eyes widen. His hair falls out. He staggers back. Both hands go between his legs. His mouth drops open. Two small round objects fall down the inside of his right pant leg and clatter to the floor, roll under the desk, plunge down a drain . . .

Meanwhile, back on the reservation, the Swampy Cree were having a party. Chief Negotiator basked in the adulation of his band members. As the leader of the Ottawa excursion, Negotiator had only a week earlier been on the edge of despair. After endless meetings, all they had come away with was a fleet of five pickup trucks from the prime minister's brother-in-law's used-car dealership.

The trucks were still in running order—more than he'd expected. Nonetheless, deep in his heart he'd known bitter disappointment.

But now, all that had changed.

Since everyone on the reservation knew that Capashin meant *sitting duck*, Chief Negotiator's plan had gone as expected: without a hitch. Now, the factory was theirs.

The party was in full swing. Cameramen from the east had come to film it for a documentary. Negotiator had explained to the interviewer that the celebration had to do with the Big Gray Buffalo That Sits On The Hill And Spews Smoke. The woman he was speaking to wrote notes with blurred hands. The band members called her *Little Capashin*. She asked about it and they told her to go to Alberta and ask the Blackfoot—they would know what it meant.

Another town meeting was called. The chambers were soon in an uproar, as villagers gathered from all parts of Capashin. His Lordship Mayor Preen arrived with a white-haired wide-eyed toothless woman they took to be his wife (whom they'd never seen, Mrs Preen never leaving the house, not even to have her hair done), and it was some time before the Mayor could convince them that the woman was Miss Minutes; and that the indoor-outdoor rug the Mayor wore on his head was a symbol of his deep-rooted conviction regarding multiculturalism, today being Hagus Day in the Hebrides.

Order restored, His Lordship Mayor Preen ascended the dais and took the podium.

"Citizens of Capashin," he began solemnly, "you all know why this meeting was called." He paused. "It would seem that the Cree have beguiled us, tricked us, deceived us, outwitted us, misconstrued us and yes, even lied to us."

"No," someone cried out from the back row.

"Yes!" Mayor Preen pounded a fist on the lectern. "They now own the hill and everything that's on it, in it, and under it. They now own—"

"The factory!" everyone yelled in unified horror.

Another voice shouted: "Mayor Preen! Are we gonna let them get away with it?"

Silence filled the chambers. Mayor Preen paused to adjust his Hagus rug. Then he leaned forward. "My fellow citizens, the agreement was signed, notarized, and witnessed. It is legally binding. Copies of it—I have been informed—have been sent to Ottawa—"

"Ottawa!"

"Yes, to Ottawa. My fellow citizens, our hands and feet are tied. The factory now belongs to the Cree."

"Wait a minute!" one voice bellowed from the crowd, and a man rose.

Miss Minutes intoned: "Council recognizes Pudge Stahlreefen."

"Yes, Pudge?" Mayor Preen prodded.

Pudge squared his shoulders, glowered about beneath enviously bushy eyebrows, and said: "I think I know somebody who's gonna have a say in this. I think we all know who that man is—"

"The Owner!" someone shouted.

Pudge nodded grimly. "The Owner. Think he's the kind of man who's gonna let a bunch of whippersnappers steal his factory right from under his nose? Hah!" Pudge sat down amidst congratulations and hearty handshakes.

Mayor Preen's eyes had narrowed at Pudge's words. In truth, he had entirely forgotten about the Owner. "Maybe," he said slowly, drawing everyone's attention back to him. "Maybe. Only," he looked around, from face to face, "anybody here ever talked to the Owner? Anybody here knows where he lives?"

Silence.

Pudge shifted in his seat, then raised a hand.

"Pudge?"

"Well, I was just thinking. Maybe we should try and find him, then."

Slowly, His Lordship Mayor Preen nodded.

They looked everywhere, but they couldn't find the Owner. They gathered at Gunrod's Cafe and drank coffee. They didn't know what else to do.

Having forded the river, Chief Negotiator rose up on his haunches and leaned out the truck window. With inscrutable eyes he looked back over his shoulder and surveyed his host, then he raised a hand into the air, held it motionless for a second, then brought it sweeping forward.

His truck in the lead, they moved out, the four Chevies fanning out behind the front-running Ford. Up ahead rose the hill, the factory long, low and gray on its summit, the smokestacks belching smoke.

Build a rocket.
Get inside.
Fire it up.
And when the prairie below is the size of a dinner plate. . .

Pudge burst into Mayor Preen's office, a mob on his heels.

His Lordship, the business end of a vacuum cleaner pressed against his temple, whirled in his chair.

"Mayor Preen! Something's happening at the factory! You better come quick!"

Hastily unplugging the vacuum cleaner, Mayor Preen leapt to his feet, donned his mayoral robes, and gestured to the door."Lead the way, Pudge."

Fattened lips and nose pressed against the porthole.
Grimacing.
Shutting off the radio that wasn't on.

Cutting in half a song that—

Bearing torches and pitchforks, the entire population of Capashin stormed towards the hill and factory. In the forefront, Mayor Preen, Miss Minutes and Pudge were the first to hear sounds of commotion. When they reached the rise and the factory came into view, they stopped as one.

Trucks, numbered five, roared circling the factory, circling the factory, circling the factory.

The Capashin mob gathered in a tight clump around Mayor Preen, who stood motionless at the summit's edge and stared bemusedly at the scene before him. Then one truck, a Ford, pulled away from the assault and approached.

"Want me to bash in its headlights?" Pudge asked Mayor Preen, hefting a club he'd found somewhere.

"No. It's Chief Negotiator."

The truck stopped. The door opened. Chief Negotiator stepped out. "All right," he growled. "What's with this factory anyway?"

"What do you mean?" Mayor Preen asked.

Negotiator turned to glare at it. "I mean, where are the doors?"

"There are no doors."

"Well, what does the factory make?"

Mayor Preen frowned. He faced his citizens. "Anybody know the answer to that one?" No one replied. Mayor Preen turned back to Negotiator and shrugged. "Don't know. Nothing ever goes in, nothing ever comes out."

"Then who the hell works there?"

"Nobody."

Chief Negotiator struggled to remain calm. "Who's the owner, then?"

Mayor Preen shrugged a second time. "Some guy. Nobody knows his name. He's hardly ever around."

"But this is crazy!"

"What is?"

"This—this whole damn thing!" Negotiator threw up his hands, whirled about and stormed back to his truck.

"Want me to bash in his taillights?" Pudge asked.

65

Mayor Preen shook his head.

"Your Hagus rug is falling off," Pudge said.

He can see his breath once every fifteen minutes. A wet sheen of white is beginning to cloud the porthole. He raises a rawhide gloved hand and turns on the defroster. The world, no bigger than a dinner plate, floats far beneath him.

The Owner adjusts some dials, pulls a few levers, leans back against the porthole and watches.

By dawn the trucks numbered five were gone. The Mayor and the mob returned to the town, dispersed to their homes, a few gathering at Gunrod's Cafe to drink coffee.

Later in the day Chief Negotiator arrived and with him was the entire band of Swampy Cree. Negotiator told Mayor Preen that he was settling his people on the hill, that they were going to be putting up houses to wait the factory out— forever, if need be. Mayor Preen gathered the townsfolk and they threw a big party to celebrate the town's 427 new citizens. The camermen and interviewer from the east packed up and went home.

Negotiator sold Mayor Preen a bottle of hair tonic after pointing out the rarity of bald Indians—the tonic was called Capashin Formula. Miss Minutes recovered her dentures at Gunrod's Cafe. Pudge was officially inducted as Chief of Police. The party lasted six days and was capped off by the appearance of a fully-haired Mayor Preen dancing arm-in-arm with Chief Negotiator.

Eventually, everyone forgot about the factory, which is still belching smoke.

People try to take him apart all the time, but they can't. In Capashin they say there's only one way to see his face. Build a rocket, get inside, fire it up. And when the prairie below is the size of a dinner plate, his face becomes visible. An eye here, another over there, and there's his grimace and French moustache, Scottish whiskers, Nordic nose, Ukrainian ears, Ojibwa eyelashes, and there—dead center in his forehead—stands the factory, belching smoke.

Revolvo

A cautionary tale
set in a city in the centre of a continent.
What follows is possibly true,
told to me—off the record—over three days
and three nights, by a cephalopod.
Never trust a writer.

PART ONE

Culture Quo

1. In which a man seeks diagnosis

Arthur Revell was fumbling with the ties of his paper shirt when the nurse stepped in.

"Have you safely stored your belongings, Mr Revell?"

Arthur squinted down at her. She was wide, full breasted, and impossibly cheerful. "Yes, Ma'am," he said. "Tell me, is your wonderful smile a job requirement, or are you truly happy with my impending predicament?"

The nurse closed Arthur's locker, removed the key and handed it to him. "It comes with the job, Mr Revell," she said, still beaming up at him. "Not to put you at ease, I'm afraid, but to keep my sanity. If you'll wait here but another moment, Dr Payne will be by shortly." She checked her pocket for her cigarettes, then left.

Arthur was alone again. He walked over to the window and looked down at the parking lot. The vehicles had backed up, filling the lanes between the rows of parked cars. Some people who had successfully parked and now wanted to drive away couldn't, while everyone else waited for spaces that didn't appear. Horns honked, two men had exited their cars and now argued, their red faces mere inches apart. Clearly, neither was a cardiac patient, since they'd been screaming at each other for some time—ever since Arthur had been led into this cramped change room by the cheery nurse.

His focus shifted as he detected something crawling on the window glass. A ladybug. Arthur was delighted. Outside, snowflakes swirled in the air, carried along by a brisk north wind that seemed to laugh at the prospects of an early spring. And here, on the seventh floor of the hospital, a ladybug meandered its way across the glass.

The curtain filling the doorway to Arthur's right was swept back and Dr Payne entered.

"Are we ready, Mr Revell?"

"Mmmm."

"Come this way, then." The doctor led him out into the hallway, speaking as he took his strange tiny steps with his strange, tiny feet. "Some patients prefer a shot of valium prior to the examination. Of course, you haven't anyone with you, so I assume you've declined the option when the nurse advised you last week—"

"Hmmm?"

"Excellent. The discomfort quickly passes, and the examination will last less than twenty minutes, provided—" the doctor turned at a doorway and looked up at Arthur over his glasses— "you relax, Mr Revell." He gestured for Arthur to enter the room. A moment later a nurse followed them inside. This one was older, her face pinched and her eyes pink with fatigue.

Dr Payne found a pair of latex gloves and put them on. He then began fidgeting over the equipment. "Enjoy your smoke, Margaret?"

The nurse placed her hands on Arthur's shoulders and guided him towards the paper-covered bench. "Each one more than the last," she answered. "Now, Mr Revell, lie down here—on your left side, please, legs tucked up, that's it, thank you. Rest your head on that towel. Excellent."

Dr Payne turned on a video monitor. "Has he been sprayed, Margaret?"

"Coming up, Doctor." The nurse leaned over Arthur. "Open your mouth, please. I'm going to spray the back of your throat with a local anesthetic. Here we go."

The spray tasted bitter, spreading numbness around his throat. At that moment, Dr Payne turned to face Arthur, in his hands a long flexible black tube as thick as a hotdog. "In this tube, Mr Revell, is a camera, a separate biopsy tube, and a suction hose."

Arthur felt drool trickle down the side of his mouth into the towel. "It's a lot bigger than the one I saw on *The Nature of Things*."

"Indeed, well, perhaps the show originated from England. They enter through the nose there, making the process quite different, sort of like right-handed driving. Of course," the doctor smiled, "we're not in England."

"That's going down my throat?"

"Coming right up. Now relax, Mr Revell. The discomfort is only momentary." The doctor inserted the tube into Arthur's mouth, reached in with his other hand and guided the blunt optic-suction-biopsy end to the back of Arthur's throat. "I am inserting now, Mr Revell. Take deep breaths and relax."

If Arthur could have spoken, he would have explained that retching spasmodically wasn't part of a devious plan to prolong the examination. As much as the doctor and the nurse cajoled him into thinking that he, Arthur Revell, was personally responsible for filling up the jar under the video monitor with his stomach fluids; that he, Arthur Revell, was contracting his stomach and duodenum to deliberately confound the camera; as much as he was made to feel guilty for not being a cadaver, there in truth was nothing he could do about his body's violent reaction to invasive examination.

He tried swallowing around the thick, hard tube, which proved his first foolish error, since the result was a succession of convulsive heaves that set the suction tube to frantic work. And once begun, there was no stopping the waves that followed.

"So far, Mr Revell," Dr Payne said ten minutes later, "I have not seen any sign of an ulcer, peptic or duodenal. As for a bacterial infection, we will of course require biopsies, which is what I will be doing now. I assure you, you won't feel a thing."

Arthur then came to the realization that Dr Payne had never had this procedure done on himself at any point in his training. The biopsies—small chunks of his stomach and middle intestine—were extracted by a metal cable with three savage teeth on its end that closed when the doctor twisted the other end. Had he been able, Arthur would have pointed out that even if he didn't have ulcers before, he did now. Each pull was a tug, a deeply felt nip, first at the furthest reach the tube could manage—far down his duodenum— somewhere under his belly button. The last biopsy was a pair of nasty nips in his esophagus. In between, the doctor removed seven more.

"Things have improved dramatically," Dr Payne assured Arthur, "now that your stomach is entirely empty. You will find yourself belching for a while, Mr Revell, since I have filled your stomach with air. I see some inflamation of the esophagus, caused by gastrointestinal fluids, but thus far it is the only indication of distress. Now, we're on our way out, Mr Revell, and it only took us, what—how long, Margaret?"

"Twenty-two minutes, Doctor."

"Very good. Very fine. Now, be certain to avoid eating or drinking for the next hour, Mr Revell. And be careful with hot fluids for an hour after that, since your throat won't be able to tell you what's too hot. Very good, Mr Revell, you did just fine."

"Use the towel to clean yourself off, Mr Revell," the nurse said. "Did you say something, Mr Revell?"

Arthur slowly sat up, wiping something that remined him of ectoplasm from his chin. "Valium," he said, "I want valium now."

The nurse scowled up at him. "Well, it's too late now, Mr Revell."

"I know," he said.

2. In which conspirators conspire

On his hands and knees, Andy "Kit" Breech followed the slime trail as it led behind the Italian leather sofa, cutting across one corner of the Kazakhstani rug, stopping at last in a circular, congealing pool in front of the balcony's sliding glass door.

"We're always squeaky clean," Annie said from the kitchen. "Always. I make sure, every time. You know me, Andy love. I make the calls. I wrap things up, right?"

Frowning, he knelt beside the gooey pool. He checked the latch and the lock. No slime there. *So, he came here to the window. But he didn't go out. He just . . . sat here. Doing what?* Andy's frown deepened, marring his usual placid, smooth expression. He studied his face reflected in the glass door. *Not good. A direct threat in the physical sense. Signs of chronic worry, fretting, uncertainty. Age I must, but those wrinkles— when they come at last— should map a lifetime of confidence, capability, efficacy. Not . . . this.*

"I mean," Annie continued, "we cleaned things up last time, didn't

71

we? The bastard still hasn't come up for air, right? Not a ripple, not one. You know me, Andy love. Uh, this is real bacon, Andy. Where's the soy bacon? I left it here last time."

"It sprouted or something," Andy muttered. He examined his reflection for a moment longer, profoundly appalled at the sheer *unease* he saw there; then his focus shifted to the balcony in the apartment block across the way. Twenty-five, maybe thirty meters distant. *What's the point of living in the penthouse when they build something even taller and stick it in your face like this? I should never have bought outright. We were culturally glutted. It was the eighties. I was young. Should've leased. I'd be in there now, right up top, my view of my city unobstructed, Instead, I'm staring at a mid-level balcony and the woman who lives in that apartment is old, age being decidedly unattractive and aesthetically disturbing. She hardly ever comes out, though, and that's good. Just her dog. It's always out. Out there right now. Hardly moving. Just sitting there staring at me. Ugly dog, too. Some kind of short-haired subcompact model. Out there day and night. Watching me. Not me, personally, of course. That would be . . . paranoid. It just looks like he's watching me. An illusion. There's no reason for him to—I never wave.*

"It's just coloured paste," Annie said. "It can't sprout."

Andy got down on his hands and knees again and began backtracking along the slime trail. "You mean it's *dead*, lovemuffin? As in deceased— expurgated—obliterated from the realm of the living?" He heard her coming from the kitchen, sensed her pausing, scanning the sunken living room, finding him nowhere.

"Where are you?" she asked, a little edgily.

"Disembodied," he said from behind the sofa. *He'd stopped here, briefly. There's tiny scratches on the floor. Evenly spaced. Make note of that.*

"Plants are lower orders of life," Annie said wearily, unable to resist the bait and knowing it. "We have to eat to survive. I refuse to see an animal killed for my sustenance. Plain and simple, Andy love, that's me. Where are you anyway?"

He crawled out from behind the sofa, carefully tracking the slime. There seemed to be another pause, just outside the closet, but he continued onward as it zigzagged from one hiding place to the next.

Annie had seen him. "Oh, God, Andy. You're getting . . . obsessed. It's kinda scary."

He scowled. *You don't know the half of it.* "You don't know him like I do," he said. "He's up to something. I can feel it."

"For godsakes get up. I've finished the salad, and the soy scramblies are done. Besides, I've got to get to the office. I called a meeting. With Lucy, and Don, and—"

"No more names," Andy said. "The less I know the better."

"What do you mean? You know everything."

"While conveying the appearance of affable, objective innocence."

"But I want to keep you informed," Annie said.

He heard the tremor in her tone. Tiny early-warning alarms chimed in his head. *Her web's trembling. Frozen in the centre, she's looking for a lifeline. Desperate is . . . unsexy. I have to think about this. Make a note. She knows I won't go down. Thinks I'm a life preserver. Mistake. Major. I want to see contingency plans asap.* "Relax," he told her, "you think I can't guess, with absolute accuracy, who'll attend this meeting of yours? Beware of conspiracies, lovetussle."

"We're not conspiring, Andy! We never do that! You know that, you know me, you know!"

"Of course not. Just a gentle reminder, darling."

Andy came to the trail's end, his eyes tracking the dried streaks climbing the metal stand, up to the double-latched, locked cover above the glass. "Perception is everything, Annie my dear." *Take my friend here, for instance. He mimicks, changes colour, changes shape even, perfectly reflecting what's in front of him. I admire that, dearest. Interesting parable, make a note for the Minister, maybe he can use it, not in public of course but for his private hate sessions. Asap.* "It counts for much, much more than reality. The world's a game of mirrors. Deflection, reflection, diffraction." He found himself eye to eye with Kit, a quarter inch of glass and a hundred million years of evolution between them. Kit wouldn't meet Andy's gaze, the eyes kept shying off to one side. His eight tentacled arms were at rest, their tips drifting lazily in the gentle current created by the water pump. Eye to eye, Kit in the shadow under the rock ledge, Andy on his knees in his penthouse. *You don't fool me, Kit. You're up to something. I don't know how you picked the lock. I don't know what you do once you're out— it's not just crawling around, oh no, there's a pattern, a purpose.* "You're a cephalopod," he whispered. "A mere octopus. Clever to be sure, with a neural sensory net more complicated and more sensitive than our own. Those tentacles, so deft, so precise—"

Annie's hands slipped over his shoulders, her fingertips inscribing patterns on his hairy chest. "Oooh," she murmured in his ear, "another fantasy. I love this bestiality stuff. You want my eight arms around you, darling? So tight they'll never let go? Hmmm?"

Andy closed his eyes. *Eight? Eight arms? See above, eg web imagery, is this coincidence? Some kind of psychic linkage? Reexamine later, make a note.* He made his sigh sound like desire. "What about your meeting?"

"It can wait," she answered huskily. "Just let me wrap my—oh-migod, look at Kit—he's frowning!"

Andy's eyes snapped open.

"Ooh now, Andy! He's going all red!"

3. Meeting the throwback

Entirely by coincidence, a certain page from a certain newspaper had been plastered on the wall by a handful of poorly rendered grease, and sat stuck there directly above Sool Koobie's tousled, burr-snagged head whenever he slept. While he couldn't read, and wouldn't have been much interested in any case, there was an article on the page discussing his existence.

One certain theory popular among some scientists held that neanderthals did not become extinct; rather, they interbred, merged with and eventually disappeared within the race of modern humans. It followed that, since these genes still persisted, there was always the chance that a perfect anachronistic match could occur within a single individual, creating a throwback. A pure, dyed-in-the-wool neanderthal, characterized by pronounced brow ridges, an oblong-shaped skull with proportionately smaller frontal lobes behind the sloping forehead, and larger occipital lobes at the back. No chin, a huge nose designed to heat glaciated air, a high and tiny larynx, a robust skeletal frame and massively large, strong muscles.

For Sool Koobie, the newspaper article on the alley wall above his nest was, could he have read it, redundant, since he himself was the real article and not in the least concerned with arguments over his existence—theoretical or otherwise.

On this particular night, in the darkness of his cave, Sool Koobie's eyes were closed, but he was wide awake. In his mind, which ran paths alien and potentially alarming to normal, modern humans, he concentrated on every detail prescribing, with absolute precision, the next few hours of his life.

He moved within his cave, alone, beyond even the suspicions of the world outside yet so intricately connected to its unmindful pulses that his hair prickled with every passage through the night's cool air, unveiling in his mind an area that extended six blocks in every direction—encompassing the heart of the city—this city. Through this mental map he danced, slipping from shadow to shadow, padding soundlessly down alleyways, pausing to test the air—nostrils flaring—and cocking his head to the sound of footsteps a block away. He gestured rhythmically with his chert-tipped spear, jabbing it as he leapt upon his unsuspecting victim. He crowed a rasping, voiceless cry, his head tilted back, as the creature stumbled and fell.

So it was, so it would be. The hunt's the thing. The hunt's this thing.

Sool Koobie knelt on the grimy floor of his cave, setting aside the weapon that would soon be slick with his victim's blood, and made propitiation to the quarry's spirit, which would flee the cooling flesh, hover uncertainly, then float away into the nightsky. Duly appeased by the respect and honour Sool was now displaying.

He opened his eyes and blinked rapidly in the musty darkness. He'd let the hearthfire dim to just a few faintly glowing coals, and now his eyes were adjusted to the night. He breathed deeply, swelling his thick, boxy chest. He jiggled his muscles loose in his arms, did the same with his short, stocky, bowed legs. He flexed and splayed out his broad, hairy toes, then finished his preparation with a twitch of his small ears.

Sool's brain was bigger than the average homo sapiens brain. Sool possessed big thoughts to match his prodigious grey matter, which is why the city was in trouble—though it knew it not.

The hunt's the thing. This thing, and another thing, soon to come.

Sool Koobie slipped outside. Within minutes he'd travelled a block, then another, moving unseen, silent and deadly. He found a hiding place, where he could wait in ambush near a watering hole, and settled in.

An hour later he rolled out from under the Cadillac, his wide, flat face smeared black with dirty oil. Heart pounding with eagerness, he sprang to his feet, straddling the curb, and sniffed deeply the night air. The rain had dampened the city's miasmic smells, but not enough to hide the scent from Sool Koobie's nose.

There were grass-eaters about, close by. A waft of weeds expelled in the breath of someone near, the slick tang of canola oil palpable on Sool's tongue. He licked his stubble-ringed lips and tested the air once more, then, hefting his spear, he slipped once again into the shadows.

4. Ambition's slow burn

Maxwell Nacht sat alone, a huge cup of decafeinated mocha lait centred on his small table, crowded against the bowl of raw sugar and the tallow candle—the huge cup his only company this night, like so many others since he'd moved to the city. The coffee had gone cold, its puff of petroleum whip collapsed into a wrinkled caldera, wax drippings from the candle abutting the cup's edge slowly flowing down, disappearing beneath the foam and secretly growing like an island on the liquid's hidden surface.

The waitress hadn't looked his way in forty minutes, so he continued his slow, rhythmic unravelling of the Peruvian straw placemat, plucking out the staples when he found them and dropping them into the golden candle's sputtering flame.

I'm in my struggling phase, Max told himself. *This is a phase in the artist's life that requires a certain amount of public display. Still, what are these staples doing in this Peruvian placemat?*

At a nearby table a conversation was underway, a smooth, oiled machine of elocution chugging along, part dialogue, part performance. Max registered every word, absorbed every nuance. He knew every person at the table, if only by reputation. They were the cream of the city's art establishment. They were brilliant. Breathtaking. Deep beyond words. They were talking.

"Can't play the game until you know the rules," Don Palmister said, shrugging ineffectually somewhere inside his sprawling carpetlike tweed jacket.

Amen to that, Alex smiled to himself.

"It's not a game," Lucy Mort said, wrinkling her nose in a way someone must have once told her was cute. "It's my life, it's what I *am,* to the very heart of my *soul.*"

"Absolutely," Brandon Safeword said, his studied enunciation delivered in a rolling tone, like ballbearings on a teak floor. "When struggle itself assumes an aesthetic modality, for instance."

A moment of silence, either in homage or bafflement—it didn't matter which, really. Talent, Max knew—*real talent—lay in mastering the ambiguity. With sufficient self-consciousness, one could turn dimwitted stupidity into an intellectual brown study.*

"In any case," Don Palmister eventually said, "it's a jungle out there, that's for certain. Clearly," the professor looked at each of his companions, "something must be done."

"Clearly," Brandon Safeword agreed. The media pundit and self-professed art critic for the Cultural Public Broadcasting station leaned back in his chair and crossed his legs. "After all, the core has begun to rot, hasn't it?"

Lucy Mort gasped.

"No," Brandon drawled, "not *that* core, darling. I was speaking of the city's core." He waved towards the restaurant's front window. "This scattering of streets, the various knots of heritage buildings presently untenanted and left to decay."

"Refurbishment," Don Palmister said, nodding. "Upscale apartments, condos, people with money . . . "

The others shared a soft laugh that made Max's stomach jump.

"Indeed," Brandon said. "Money."

Everyone laughed again, the magic word even better the second time around.

A distant shriek from somewhere outside made Max sit up, alarmed. He twisted in his seat and leaned close to the window. Outside, all he could see was the wet street, parked cars and old, exhaust-stained buildings. *Must've been a car. Of course it was a car. Whew.* He sat back. No one else had heard the sound, it seemed. Unnerving, sitting this close to the dark world outside, but it had been the last table available.

Culture Quo Vegetarian Restaurant was a popular place.

"I've found," Don Palmister was saying, "that the postmodernistic zeitgeist has finally embraced the culminating notion of dismantled meaning." He paused to roll his eyes and shift again inside his tweed jacket. "It's been a notion of mine, firmly implanted in my class syllabi for at least ten years."

Syllabi? Like . . . octopi? Of course there's no such word as octopi. The word is octopod. Syllapod, a many-tentacled description swathed in a cloud of black ink when alarmed.

"Patience," Brandon said. "The ultra-awareness of pure genius, once delivered into the virgin and perhaps limited minds of your students, professor, necessitates a certain gestation period before fruition, hah hah, ho ho!"

"Sure, Brandon," Don said, "but where's my credit?"

Everyone laughed again, but this time the sound had acquired a timbre of uncertainty. Said in jest or honest vexation—that seemed to be the secret question.

Whining's always honest, Max nodded to himself. *But very artfully done, Professor Palmister. You've got them guessing.*

The conversation ended abruptly, as did the serene hum of a healthy dining experience, when the door banged open and two young men stumbled inside, faces white and eyes wide with fear—Max hadn't even seen them coming, but he shrank back from the chill air that swept in around them. The two men skidded to a stop just inside the door, heads whipping as they stared wildly at everyone in the restaurant.

"Someone help us!" the man closest to Max screamed. "Our friend's been attacked!"

"Kidnapped!" the other shouted.

"This hairy naked man jumped us from an alley!"

"He had a spear—he stuck it in Maury!"

"Maury's our friend!"

"Maury fell down and the naked guy barked at us—"

"Snapped and showed his teeth!"

"Then he dragged Maury into the alley!"

"Someone call the police!"

"We're regular patrons here!"

"Maury, too!"

Brandon Safeword surged to his feet, his massive, muscular frame suddenly dominating the room. "My God," he whispered, "not again!"

5. Lessons in history

Joey "Rip" Sanger's mother threw herself in front of a train the day his father walked out on them. It had been one of those vintage jaunts somewhere around the Gatineau Hills, a Kitson Meyer steam engine pulling six antique smokers full of Health Club Americans on a package tour. She'd stepped between the restored Bullhead rails at a sharp bend from which, on a clear day and with the aid of binoculars, one could see Ottawa.

The Kitson Meyer had slowed to a steady twenty miles an hour taking the bend, and the broad cow-catcher scooped up Joey's mother and gave her a three-hour ride down into Hull. She'd walked away with only a chipped front tooth which she got when she rolled off the catcher at the station.

These days, Emilia Sanger knitted toques for old folks in Scarborough.

Joey's father had gone off to find his true love. Five years later Joey and his brothers received a photograph postcard showing their old man, his white face a startling blotch amidst all the dark-skinned Pakistanis, perched on the runner of the twelfth Clayton Wagon steamer originally built in Lancashire. Most historians claimed that the Clayton Wagon Company built only eleven engines. Thomas Sanger had found his phantom lover, doing the Afghanistan run, and on the back of the card he'd written: *Go get 'em, boys.*

A sentiment his three sons had taken to heart. Wally Sanger, the eldest, was doing time in Fort Saskatchewan for the attempted murder of their kid brother, Mack. Wally had been a professional scab for the railroad companies. Mack had gotten in the way on a picket line and Wally had driven over him, crushing both legs and leaving him a paraplegic. They'd since patched things up and now wrote each other every other day.

Like his brothers, like his old man and his grandfather and his great-grandmother on daddy's side, the railroad was in Joey's blood. His grandfather, Straight-line Sanger, drove the third to last spike in the Rockies moments before pitching over dead of heat prostration and, it was rumoured, syphilis. Joey's great-grandmother, Liza Sanger, baked bread, built saunas and stored explosives for the railroad work teams at the camp southwest of Rennie. One day, while walking beside a stone house—which held seven hundred and seventy-seven sticks of dynamite—Liza had blown up. Not the house. Just her. Stories went around after that, since everybody knew how Liza had an adventurous spirit.

Joey "Rip" Sanger stepped off the train at the station and waited for the Red Cap to collect his twin steel trunks from the baggage car. He ran a battered hand across his fiery red brush-cut, scratched at his scar, then fished for a fiver from his off-white trenchcoat's spacious pockets. The Red Caps had a history. Something that demanded respect. The fiver would tell this Red Cap that Joey knew what tradition was all about.

He watched the crimson-clad young man loading the twin steel trunks onto the roller. The man wheeled the cart up to Joey. "Man, these are heavy buggers, Jack. Whatcha got in 'em, rocks?"

Joey scowled. "Red Caps bend their backs without jawing and moaning. Red Caps don't retire. They go on compensation. You new or something, son?"

"Tell ya what, Jack. You just climb on here and I'll roll ya all off the ramp and the Devil with ya."

"Follow me to the head office. I got an appointment."

"You gonna citation me?"

Joey turned away and headed for the hallway that led into the company offices. He pulled out the fiver and fluttered it over one shoulder. "Let's go, Bobby-boy, we're wasting time and Joey "Rip" Sanger never—I repeat, never—wastes time."

"Did you say Joey "Rip" Sanger? Geez, Mister Sanger, I didn't know, honest. I'm right with ya, Mister Sanger, right here behind ya. Y'just lead the way and I'm right with ya."

They passed through the room containing the scaled-down model reconstruction of the station yards. Joey waved a hand at it. "This, Bobby-boy, is something you should pay attention to. It's what we're all about and you know why?" He paused at the door and met the Red Cap's wide eyes.

"No," the young man said softly.

"Cause it's for the little people, that's why."

They continued on, came to a stop outside the president's office. "Leave the trunks here," Joey said.

"Yessir, Mister Sanger. And I'll stand guard, too, right here till you're done."

Joey narrowed his iron-grey eyes to slits. "Learn to respect that red cap, son." He raised the five-dollar bill. "Learn it good, and maybe one day a fiver like this one will land in your pocket." He swung around, opened the door and stepped inside the office.

Joey hung up his trenchcoat, scrubbed the crimson bristle on his head, then walked past the secretary. "Wild Bill in, honey? Good, I ain't got much time. Buzz him I'm on my way, let's see how fast you are." He walked to the inner door and had his hand on the knob before the secretary suddenly snatched at the intercom on her desk. Joey grinned to himself and stepped into the president's office.

"G'afternoon, scum-face," he said to the balding man spread out in the chair behind an antique desk. "Hey, you're not Wild Bill Chan. What the hell you doing in his chair? Take a hike, I got an appointment with Chan."

The balding man's round, patchy face deepened a shade as he slowly sat forward. "You got one thing right, Mister Sanger," he said in a reedy voice. "Wild Bill made the call, making sure it was you who'd take the job. But he retired last year. The name's Jeremy Under. Please, Mister Sanger, take a seat."

Scowling, Joey sat down. "What the hell? Wild Bill couldn't be over eighty-five. What do you mean, he retired?"

"It was," Jeremy Under said, "a forced retirement. Management folded on this one, because it had to. The old give and take. We fold, they fold, you know how it is. Now, onto the business at hand." The man leaned back, lacing his pudgy fingers together on his round belly. "The reports have it you almost single-handedly collared that Kerouac Gang out of Toronto's East Side."

"No 'almost' about it, Blotto," Joey said. "Those punks have hopped their last free ride."

Jeremy Under's eyes bugged out. "What did you call me?" he squeaked.

"What's the matter? Got a thin skin? Get outa the business if you do. Ain't no room for beached whales who can't even sit up straight. Now, I got nothing against being fat. Mack's turned into a walrus since he got his legs cut off. Just carry it right, will ya? That's all it takes. Some pride in yourself. You got the mass, but you ain't got the moxy, if you know what I mean. Takes a little practice, that's all. Now, what's all this about a bunch of homeless scrubs squatting on railroad property? Sounds like a minor infestation, I'd think you prairie boys could've handled it— not that it matters anymore. I work alone. I'll scrape your lands clean, or I'm not Joey 'Rip' Sanger." He stood, reached up and traced a blunt, stained finger along the scar running diagonally over his eyebrows. "Now, if you can lever that disgusting bulk outa the chair, show me your track maps. What the hell you waiting for, ten Red Caps with crowbars?"

Joey walked out of the office and collected his trenchcoat. As he put it on he turned to the gaping, wide-eyed secretary. "Better call an ambulance, honey. Your boss ain't looking too good. Burst blood vessel, I'd guess. Only a matter of time when you let yourself go like that, of course. Let me know when's the funeral, I'll send a card. Now, where's the survey maps of the company yards? I've got work to do."

PART TWO

The Peers

1. In which the diagnosis is revealed

The cheerful nurse led Arthur to an alcove at one end of the Recovery Room. It was opposite the nurse station and had a loveseat sofa and a recliner. Behind the sofa was a large window with all its seams and joins painted over, a window never meant to be opened, but the spring sun's midday light was welcome all the same.

"Dr Payne will be with you shortly," the nurse said. Under her lab coat she wore a blouse with a surprisingly low neckline. She'd been taking her coffee breaks outside, Arthur concluded, since her chest was bright pink. The curiously alluring blush above her deep cleavage made Arthur think of sunny dispositions. He smiled down at her, then slowly sat in the recliner, reaching for a magazine from the stack on the end table.

He began reading an article randomly chosen from the magazine and within moments was engrossed in a theoretical battle between two camps of economists as they advanced fiscal projections into the next decade. He felt a twist or two of envy reading about business executives and investment portfolios—the same kind of vague yearning he sometimes experienced when walking down a street and seeing all the brand new cars rolling past. It baffled him how so many people could have so much money . . . especially given the dire economic forecasts and the shapeless, invisible but terribly heavy cloud of national debt under which he and everyone else in the country laboured—the very debt the article in the magazine was going on and on about.

"Ah, Mr Revell."

Arthur looked up to find Dr Payne standing in front of him. "My goodness," Arthur said, "you look very tired, Doctor. Please, sit down." He indicated the loveseat as he returned the magazine to the stack on the end table.

"Tired?" Dr Payne's eyebrows rose, then dropped. "Indeed, I suppose I am." He sat down. "Of course, aren't we all these days, hmm?"

"I feel quite well rested, actually," Arthur said. "If not for the national debt, I might well consider my life worry-free. Tell me, Doctor, is it possible I have a national ulcer? What I mean is, could I be suffering the stress of *the citizen*, you know, something representational of high unemployment, declining social services, hiring inequities, escalating prices and so on? Or is it the plight of youngish folk in modern society? Are these things even possible, Doctor?"

"Assuming a massive neurosis on your part, Mr Revell, anything is possible." The doctor cleared his throat, glanced out the window. "Mind you, I found no ulcer." He looked back at Arthur and smiled. "Are you a collector, by any chance? I've been for a long time. Porcelain figures from England. Very therapeutic. My hedgehog collection is insured by Lloyd's, which in some circles doesn't mean as much as it used to, given the declining reputation of insurance industries the world over. In any case, what were we talking about?"

"This is my follow up to the internal examination," Arthur said. "Even so, do you concur that the decline of the insurance industry is simply a symptom of an overall loss of faith in the market system?"

"I certainly hope not!" Dr Payne said, laughing. "What would be the point of my owning a BMW and a Jaguar if all distinctions should suddenly vanish? In such a world, Mr Revell, I envision the nightmare where I am the patient and you the doctor, if you see what I mean."

"No."

"Well, never mind that. Our biopsies indicate that, indeed, you are infected with a nasty, very pervasive bug. It will require treatment, beginning immediately."

"A bug?"

"Hundreds of millions of them, in fact. Of the family *Aphidae*, having a soft, pear-shaped body and a tube-shaped mouth. Even at this moment, as we speak, they devour at your insides. This is why it is paramount we begin treatment immediately. You are, Mr Revell, being quietly ingested."

"What a distressing thought," Arthur said.

"No doubt." DrPayne reached into his coat pocket and withdrew a cellular phone. "Excuse me while I take this call."

Arthur blinked. He'd heard no ring. He watched as DrPayne activated the phone and held it to his ear, his frown deepening as the seconds ticked by.

"You want me in Entymology," the doctor said, nodding. "Third floor, yes of course. Containment Room B, yes." He sat up straight. "My God, not Room B! I'll be right there!" The doctor rose, looking momentarily lost.

"My treatment," Arthur prompted.

"Hmm? Oh, yes." DrPayne pulled out a pill bottle. "Take three of these every four hours. See the nurse for more details. I must be off. Excuse me, Mr Revell. And do let me know if you see any hedgehogs, hmm? Goodbye."

Arthur watched him leave. He glanced down at the bottle in his hand, hesitating as a part of him wanted to return to the article in the magazine. Of course, that wasn't proper form. He climbed to his feet and approached the nurse's station.

The cheerful nurse had gone to look at one of the patients in the beds in the recovery room, leaving the older nurse, Margaret, behind the desk. Arthur leaned on the counter. "Excuse me, Ma'am. DrPayne directed me here to get details of the medication he's putting me on."

Margaret coughed then held out her hand. "Let's see the bottle, Mr Revell."

He passed it over.

She read the label, "125 mg, Coccinellidae, hmmm, not one I'm familiar with." She jotted the name down on a notepad. "Well, take three at a time every four hours. You have three refills on this prescription, to be dispensed by DrPayne's clinic. There are three hundred pills inside. Anything else you want to know, Mr Revell?"

"I'm to take nine hundred pills?"

Margaret frowned slightly and reread the label. "Yes, Mr Revell, that's correct."

"Well," Arthur said, "he *is* the doctor, isn't he?"

"Correct, Mr Revell. Now, if you haven't anymore questions, I'm about to go on my coffee break."

"By all means," Arthur said. "Enjoy your cigarette."

"Each one more than the last, Mr Revell. Thank you. You can find your own way out?"

"Oh yes."

Arthur continued smiling as he watched Margaret leave the room. After a moment he glanced down at himself, making sure his fly was zipped and nothing was out of place. He ran both hands through his reddish-brown hair, rubbed a finger over his teeth, then turned to watch the cheerful nurse.

She was still busy, arguing with an enormous, balding man occupying a bed halfway down the aisle. The man looked very angry, the colour of his face alarmingly red as he bellowed incomprehensible orders into his cellular phone. The cheerful nurse was still smiling, but it was clear to Arthur that even she was losing her patience as she tried to calm the patient down.

Arthur walked over. "Do you require assistance, Ma'am?" he asked.

"Mr Revell!" The nurse's own face was now flushed, almost the same tone as her chest. "Thank you for asking, but I'm afraid it's against hospital policy to enlist the aid of patients when restraining other patients. Insurance, you understand."

Arthur smiled, his head bobbing. "I understand perfectly. Of course, in some circles, the insurance industry has a very poor reputation. I therefore suggest we ignore such concerns for the time being." He walked over to stand beside the patient's bed, gently guiding the nurse to one side. "Sir?" he asked the man, who made a point of ignoring Arthur. "Sir, I suggest you calm down immediately. Please end your phone-call and comply with the nurse's instructions."

The man laid a hand over the phone's mouthpiece and glared up at Arthur.

"Get outa my goddamned face," he snapped in a high, quavering voice. "I'll sue the lot of you, I swear. I'm *cardiac*, you idiots. Not gastrointestinal! Cardiac! What the hell's wrong with all of you, anyway? Get me outa here!"

Arthur's smile tightened slightly. "Sir, kindly look at this patient here beside you. Is he raving at the top of his lungs? No, he isn't. In fact. he's trying to get some sleep—"

"Of course he's not screaming his head off," the balding man yelped. "Someone stuck a spear into his belly! Wouldn't you be lying low, too?"

"Please, Mr Revell," the nurse said, moving close and making an effort to guide him away from the bedside. She smelled of peaches. "I will be calling for assistance—"

"Nonsense," Arthur said. He leaned over the bed and looked down at the balding man. "I'm about to throw up. Stress induces vomiting, you see, and I'm finding you very stressful, Sir. My concern is that I have in my stomach a hundred million *aphidae,* voracious little bugs that can only be treated with nine hundred pills. Now, I wouldn't want you to contract this terrible affliction, but your constant screaming at that poor beleaguered secretary on the other end of the phone line has my stomach rumbling in a most ominous fashion."

The balding man cringed. "Get away from me" he said in a tiny voice.

"I'm afraid it may be too late," Arthur said, still looming over the man. "Unless you hang up immediately."

The man switched off his phone and shoved it into the nurse's hands.

"Ahh," Arthur said, stifling a burp. "That's much better."

"You're insane," the man said.

"Possibly I am," Arthur replied. "I hadn't considered that. Of course, I have received my diagnosis, thank goodness, and medication to remedy my condition. Additional ills are of course possible." He turned to the nurse. "What do you think, Ma'am? Might I also be insane as well as gastrointestinally infected?"

She smiled, taking his arm by the elbow and guiding him away. "Not likely, Mr Revell. Thank you for helping—you certainly have a presence, don't you?"

"My robustness hasn't always served me as well," Arthur said. "And lately I seem to be gaining weight without accumulating any extra fat—is this possible? Is my flesh becoming denser?"

"I have no idea, Mr Revell."

They were standing at the nurse's station. The nurse's blue eyes were searching his, as if seeing him for the first time.

"I wonder," Arthur began tremulously, "uhm, a certain thought has occurred to me—"

"Oh?" Her eyes had widened.

"Well, I wonder if you might not consider it too forward of me to ask you out on a date, as it were. Dinner, perhaps?"

"I don't know if that's such a good—"

"Strictly speaking, I'm not your patient, am I?"

"True. Oh, why not? Yes, I'd like that."

"Uh, may I ask your name, Ma'am?"

"Faye."

"How charming, Faye. Tomorrow night, then?"

"I get off at seven," she said.

"I'll be here."

Down on the main floor, Arthur went into the bathroom and shook out three of the pills. He squinted down at the red, black-spotted objects. Each pill seemed to be cut in a half—hemispherical. He shrugged, popped them into his mouth, and swallowed. It was a great relief that his treatment had begun. Smiling, Arthur left the hospital.

2. "You're our man, Max!"

Outré Space, the hub of the city's art establishment, was a beautiful old building designed and constructed in the Chicago style of the early 1900s. It had been gutted and refurbished to become a kind of self-contained focal point, housing arts associations, studios, a cinema, and countless other arts-related stuff.

As with every time he entered Outré Space, Maxwell Nacht paused in the foyer, his skin prickling, the hairs erect on the back of his neck, and fighting the sudden urge to vacate his bowels. The reaction was triggered by the building itself, rather than the lofty organizations it housed. In truth, he was anticipating the scene to come, knowing he would be taking a massive risk, but confident in his choice of tactics.

Four ceiling-mounted security cameras swivelled in their brackets to focus on him. He'd already stepped through the infrared sensor beam at the doors, and the foyer still echoed from the Door Open chime.

I don't belong here. Yet.

Heavy boots echoed, approached with the rustle of cloth and the clink and soft jangle of metal.

I'm an intruder at this moment, shifty, potentially loitering, a shabby beggar in student-budget clothes, my hair misaligned by the endless wind outside and now slowly settling at the front, above my sweat-beaded brow, but rising distinct and erect at the back—charged by the oven-dry air. An intruder. Desperate. Psychotic. An artist.

The security guard arrived. Max read the name tag on the man's flak vest: Monk. With the black, face-shielded helmet, only the name tag distinguished one from the others—and there were at least two more. Max had encountered Stubble yesterday, and Nick the day before. They all wore the helmets, the fatigues, the web belt with gas grenades, and the M-16s slung over their shoulders, one gloved hand on the butt of the Service .45 at their hips. They were all big, blockish, silent.

Max smiled. "How's Stubble and Nick? Doing well, are they?"

Monk stared at him.

"Uh," Max continued, "I have an appointment with Annie Trollop, CAPSs. Uh, Cultural Assessment Promotional Support services. Fifth floor, Room 500. One p.m. I know, I'm six minutes early, but—"

Monk gestured him towards the elevator. Its doors opened as soon as they arrived and they didn't pause in their step until they entered and the doors closed behind them.

A corner-mounted ceiling camera swivelled its eye in his direction. A speaker grille beside the floor button panel buzzed, then a voice said, "The elevator will take you directly to the required floor. Speak clearly in stating your floor."

"Uh, five," Max said.

"The elevator will take you directly to floor five. There is no reason to panic."

Panic?

"I, uh, I need to go to the bathroom." He checked his watch as the elevator began climbing. "I have four minutes . . . "

There was silence, then, "Use of bathrooms is discouraged."

"Oh."

"Unless accompanied by security."

The elevator stopped, presumably at the fifth floor, but the doors remained closed.

"Okay . . . " Max said slowly.

"Proceed then."

The doors opened. Max stepped into a hallway. Monk trundled after him, one step behind his left shoulder. The elevator said, "The guard will accompany you."

"Okay. Got it."

"Do not deviate from the route."

"Right."

Monk gesturing the direction, they began walking. They turned right, then right again, passing unmarked, unnumbered and closed doors on either side of the hallway, and finally came to a stop outside yet another featureless, steel-grey door. As Maxwell stared at it the doorknob buzzed and clicked open.

Monk followed him into the bathroom and into the stall. Max hesitated, wondering if he could manage to poo with Monk standing beside him. He jumped as the toilet said, "You may now sit. This is stall Alpha Charlie. This is your stall for the duration of your stay. If questioned, you are in Alpha-Charlie-5. Do you understand?"

"Yes, Sir."

"You may now sit."

"Sit?'

"Shit."

"Thank you."

Brief interlude

The damp from Annie's limp hand still cooling on Maxwell's palm, he sat down in the chair indicated and smiled at the pretty-but-too-thin woman on the other side of the desk.

"Boy," Maxwell said, "the security here in Outré Space is state-of-the-art stuff. I'm, uh, very impressed."

Annie Trollop smiled without showing her teeth. "Yes, very impressive, I'm sure. Are you new to the city? I see you've but recently joined CAPSs, Mr Nacht."

"Max, please. Yes. I'm from . . . out of town. A rural upbringing." He raised his hands in a slightly-helpless-but-restrained-by-decorum gesture, which he'd worked on all morning in his small apartment, to an audience of cockroaches on the kitchen counter. "I admit to experiencing . . . culture shock. What most excites me," he continued, "is this notion—ably described in your information pamphlet—of a true, vibrant, thriving arts community. Does such a community exist?"

A brief frown flickered on Annie's brow. "Which one?"

"Excuse me?"

"Which information pamphlet?"

"Uhm, uh, I'm not sure—you have more than one?"

"Oh, yes, a series, each one target-specific. We've spent thousands researching and producing our pamphlets. Let's see, the arts community . . . vibrant, thriving, you said? Well, that would be Series 16-B—you got the pamphlet for potential donors. You should have received Series 11-D, for new members." She shook her head and sighed. Picking up a pen and making a note she said, "Well that does it. She's fired. I simply cannot deal with this level of incompetence. Series 11-D is for new members—she should know that."

"So, I'm curious, how's it different?"

"Well, in Series 11-D the arts community is 'welcoming, appreciating, open and receptive.' "

"Oh. Seems a small mistake—"

"Hardly, Mr Nacht. Now, where were we?"

He hesitated, then said, "I was enthusing about there being an arts community and displaying appropriate eagerness, intending to convey to you my eager willingness to do anything it takes to become part of that community."

"Ah, excellent, Maxwell. I must say, I'm impressed. Do you have any opinions?"

"No, none at all, and I don't make them."

"Superb. Do you consider yourself an ethical person? Do you have standards?"

"No, I'm completely amoral. All art produced by notable members of the community is either 'good' or 'interesting.' "

"Are you cynical?"

"To the black core of my rotten heart."

Annie Trollop leaned back, looking thoughtful. "The timing is . . . propitious. We need a new wunderkind. Someone we can milk and glom and flutter and sigh over—for a year, maybe two. Then we'll get tired and move on." She looked at Max. "A year, maybe two, Maxwell."

"Sounds perfect," he replied. "I won't fail you, and I won't hang on after it's over."

"Well I should think not, Mr Nacht. Because then you'll join that elite, powerful group—you'll become a—"

"A peer."

"Exactly."

He smiled.

She smiled back. "We've found our boy. Now, let's go. Introductions of the proper sort need to be made."

"Wonderful."

"Have you visited Anything But Craft?"

"Your retail outlet? No, it never seems to be open—"

"Well of course not. Heaven forbid we actually *sell* something. Because then someone would be unfairly favoured over others, and that's not allowed. But come, I'm certain Penny is in."

Max stood. "Penny? Penny Foote-Safeword? Brandon Safeword's wife?"

"Exactly. We'll explain everything, and she'll get to work. You're about to enter the revolving door, Maxwell—no, not Maxwell. Maximillian. Maximillian Percival Nacht, I think."

They headed out.

"Revolving door?"

"Oh yes, our, shall we say, euphemism. The track, the pathway. Grants, awards, a lifetime of funding. Round and round and round. Once you're in the loop, you never have to come out, you see. And of course there's no official way to get into the loop in the first place. It's the way of modern life, Maximillian, it's—"

"Revolvo."

"Precisely. Very apt. How clever. Follow me . . . "

They left Annie's office, walked past the luckless underling who was destined for firing, headed out into the hallway—where Monk was nowhere in sight—then descended five flights of stairs, proceeded along another hallway, and came at last to a featureless steel door. "This is the back way into the studio area of the shop," Annie explained. "It's necessary that you memorize the floorplans of the building, since it is deliberately intended to confuse and, indeed, lose the uninitiated. We've had three would-be-artists disappear in Outré Space over the past five years. Stubble swears he's seen one of them, but somehow, the cameras never detect him, or her, or them." She turned to the door and knocked. After a moment she produced a key and opened the door. "Penny!" she called. "Darling! We have a guest!"

They edged inside.

Penny was lying on a kind of divan at the opposite end of the studio. Paint-spattered cloth had been draped and tacked to the wall behind and to either side of her. Bits of tinfoil hung from threads attached to the ceiling and slowly turned in the warm, incense-sweet air. A videocamera mounted on a tripod was off to one side, a red light blinking on it.

Max had never seen Penny before, and in fact knew almost nothing about her, except that she was Brandon Safeword's wife. As he and Annie approached, he saw that the woman, in her early forties, was dressed in a see-through, tye-dyed kind of slip that outlined her body without providing any support. Her breasts were large and hadn't known a bra in years. Bits of bark and leaves were profligate in her long black hair. Her red-painted lips were huge although the rest of the face was narrow, modestly featured, and her catlike eyes, lined in kohl, stayed mostly hidden under the painted lids.

"Oh, Annie dear," she purred—well, Max corrected in his mind, it was meant to be a purr, but the sound had come mostly from her nose. "You've found me my installation piece, I see."

Annie waved a hand. "This is Maximillian Nacht, honey. Our new boy. He's destined for moderately great things."

"An artist?" Penny let her gaze rest on Max. "And what do you do, Maximillian Nacht?"

"Uh, I'm a sculptor."

"Call me Penny."

"Penny."

"And what do you sculpt?"

"Everything. I mean, anything. I'm presently doing miniatures."

"How economical." Penny glanced at Annie and raised her thin eyebrows.

"Well," Annie smiled, "I'd best be off. Office work, how it piles up. Maximillian, I leave you in capable hands. Pay close attention to what Penny tells you, and you'll do just fine."

"Thanks, Annie."

The chief administrator for CAPSs closed the door behind her, leaving Max alone with Penny.

"Well, come closer, my bite's not too painful," Penny said. "Have you read my book?"

"Uhm, no I'm sorry, I haven't."

"That's not surprising. I refused to let crass commercial retail outlets sell it. Self-published, too, since why should some faceless publishing company profit from my efforts. So, you can only acquire the book from moi, which is perfect, for it allows me, the author, to elect my own audience—an exclusive one, an audience worthy of my work."

"That's very clever, Penny."

"Of course," Penny said, "you're now among that elite company, so I'll have to find a copy, sometime, somewhere."

"What's the book called?"

Her smile made Max's heart jump—or maybe it was his liver, the incense was putting him in a daze. "Is the videocam on?"

He stumbled over to the tripod. "Uh, yep, it's running."

"What do you know about performance art, sweetie?"

"Not much, I'm afraid."

"Uninitiated, then. Excellent. I'm working on a project that is a continuation of the book, an expansion of the basic precepts. Research is paramount. Come here, take off your clothes."

"My clothes?"

"We're going to fuck. A performance piece, art in all its visceral glory. I have made a discovery—it's all in my book—and it's revolutionary, it might well change the world forever. Have you ever heard of collective memory?"

"As in Carl Jung?"

"Someone like that—I can't recall, but that doesn't matter. What's important to realize is that this collective memory is not found in the brain. Oh no, darling, not the brain. Take off your clothes, Maximillian, and get over here. We're wasting tape. Where was I?"

Max began stripping down. "Anywhere but the brain," he said.

"I have discovered it is possible to tap into that memory, to unveil the mysteries of all one's past lives, the myriad identities of one's genetic histories. For example, I have discovered that I was once a princess, no twice, once in Egypt, and once at Stonehenge. I have also been a queen, a high priestess, and an amazon warrior. These identities can be driven back into my consciousness, because, as the title of my book reveals, *The Vulva Remembers!*" With that she lunged forward, wrapping Max in her arms and pulling him down onto the divan. "Fuck me fuck me fuck me—she'll remember again, ohmigod, she'll remember—she remembers!"

3. The ends of the line

Wild Bill Chan hobbled along the abandoned rail line, dragging one leg that had been crushed in 1962 at a spill outside Climax, Saskatchewan, walking with a rolling hitch of his hunched back, which had been bent and then broken in 1969 trying to hold up a derailed, sagging-in-the-mud piggyback just outside Ste Rose du Lac, Manitoba. He glared at the world with one eye, the other one lost in 1974 when he was trampled by a herd of caribou being pursued by a polar bear down Churchill's main street—his only off-duty injury in a long list of injuries that had begun in 1920 when, as a mere lad, he had joined his father on the crew breaking the path for the northern line.

Joey "Rip" Sanger grinned as the old man approached. "Hell, getting ya outa that damned retirement weren't too hard, eh?" Behind Joey stood the Red Cap, who'd had a hell of a time dragging one of the steel trunks out to this forgotten spur. He'd damned near earned his fiver, Joey reflected. Almost. The prairie spread out beyond the line, dotted here and there by derelict grain silos and bought-out farmsteads. A few dusty trees broke the flat skyline to the east and north, while to the south rose the city's scattering of skyscrapers, behind a golden veil of spring dust.

Chan arrived and hooked his glare up at Joey. "Y'bastard," he rasped. "Eh was 'alfway t'Katmandu when the call come."

"Under was under the weather, hah," Joey said. "Thin skin and too much under it, if you ask me. This the guy you groomed to take over, Chan? Hell, what a sorry thought."

"Times change, Joey. That's all eh say. So you call me out here, y'grizzled carp, but in case y'hadn't noticed, this spur's abandoned." He waved a mangled hand in a sweeping gesture. "'Alf the track's rusting t'nothing, boy! The heydey's scrammed. It was the twenties, the best times, when it was touch and go between this city and Chicago and St Louis—who was going to be the gate to the west, hey? Touch and go. You'll find more track round this city than y'can fathom, boy, round and round and round. Spurs and runs and switchbacks and platforms and silos and maintenance shacks and sheds and damned cars, too, boy!"

Joey grimaced. "You forget, you one-eyed Shanghai warlock, you're talking to Joey 'Rip' Sanger here. Y'think I can't read maps, y'think two thousand miles of unused track around this city is enough to make my knees shake?" He kicked at the rail. "Unused, hell. Take a close look, Chan."

"Eh?"

"Your squatters are living in cars, got their own goddamned train, look where the rust's streaked away. Looking pinched, right? It's a 57 Wells, a goddamned steam engine. Not listed on your service, is it? But it's here, and someone's working it, and those squatters are living in the cars behind it, and they got you hunting everywhere but so long as they keep to the abandoned spurs, so long as they keep moving, you won't find 'em."

"Holy bear livers," Chan whispered.

"You got it. It's bloody ingenious. I can't wait to meet the brains behind it all, and mark you, Chan, I will. Soon. The bastard's mine, all mine. Red Cap!"

"Yes sir!"

Joey tossed the boy a ring of keys. "Open that trunk, son."

The Red Cap fumbled through the keys, and finally found the right one. He lifted back the hinge, then stepped back.

Joey and Chan walked up to the trunk. Inside was a sophisticated array of hi-tech equipment, motion sensors, IR sensors, and innumerable other gadgets of detection and tracking, all neatly stored in stacked foam beds. Joey said to Chan, "I want a two-man runner brought here. We've got a whole lotta lines to seed before dark."

"Ground up dragon bones," Chan swore, "you'll get what you need, Joey."

"What was that about Katmandu, anyway?"

"Got part-time work as a Sherpa. But never mind, I want to see you nab these squatters. The old glory's back, Joey. You're a goddamned wonder, boy." Chan faced the Red Cap and scowled up at the young man. "You stick by him, son, and you'll learn something, you'll learn enough to carry on the tradition—and someday you'll be running this goddamned company!"

"Yes sir!"

Chan said to Joey, "You gonna sock it to'em, ain't ya?"

Joey paused over the trunk and cocked his head. "The Sanger Sock? If I have to, I suppose. Better they come along peacefully, though."

"The Sanger Sock?" the Red Cap asked.

Chan nodded. "A martial art, a single move no one on earth has stood against, and that includes Clay himself—was in '63, in Toronto, at a house-party in Don Mills. Things got rough between Joey and the Champ." Chan cackled. "The Yank got whupped by a Canuck! Again! Hee hee!" He continued after a moment, "Of course they hushed it up. Bad press and all that. The Sanger Sock, first invented by Liza Sanger, when she was working in the bush on the Rennie crew—all those horny

Finns, hah! Then passed down the line, all the way to Joey here."

"Wow," the Red Cap breathed. "Can I learn it?"

"Mind your manners, boy," Joey snapped. "You're getting uppity."

"Nothing wrong with that, Joey," Chan said. "A kid's gotta be uppity, wants to get anywhere."

"S'pose you're right. Well, you gotta earn the right, Red Cap. I seen signs, good signs, I admit. We'll see, I s'pose. Now, give me a hand here and Chan, you ain't that well-hung so I figure that's a cellular in that pocket, so put in the call for that two-man runner."

Chuckling, Chan reached into his pants pocket.

4. Anything but craft

After the taping they went to another taping, this one somewhat more sedate. Penny was in a fine mood, still swimming in the euphoria of discovering an Aztec princess in one of her past lives. Max, on the other hand, could barely walk.

"I'm the producer," Penny said as they stood in the foyer and waited for the elevator. "The *Northern Order Program* is not only the premiere quality show on the arts in this city, it's the only show on the arts in this city. Brandon is, of course, simply superb. Not that I'm biased. My objectivity in all things is above reproach. In any case, we're taping this week's show at Art Place Gallery, which is just upstairs." She checked her watch. "Everything should be set up by now. Excellent. Ideal. Karmic synchronicity. Don't worry, I'll make introductions."

The elevator arrived. They entered. "Second floor," Penny said loudly. The speaker grille chirped, and they ascended.

Most of the second floor was taken up with the public gallery—although, as the sign posted on the door indicated, it wasn't open to the public. "Art Place Gallery," Penny explained, "is for our darling artists, the prize students of important people. In order to get a show in here—which can be seen by invitation only—you must have studied under professor Don Palmister, or Lucy Mort. You must receive a letter of reference from my dear husband, and a personal nonwritten reference from moi."

"Oh," said Max. "But I haven't studied under either Don or Lucy."

"Don't worry about that, Maxie. There are always ways around the rules. Always. Besides, Annie's backing you, and that should open all the doors. Also," she smiled demurely, "you have moi in your camp. Not to be too immodest, you can't lose. Ah, here we are."

They entered into the spacious gallery. The TV camera was already set up, a technician perched behind it. Brandon Safeword had taken position, the tips of his shoes perfectly aligned with two strips of white tape on the hardwood floor, beside a huge, imposing work of art.

Max gaped at it as he and Penny approached. The work of art was a cow, stuffed, legs spread out, tail sticking straight out, and an SLR camera jammed into its mouth. A black box had been strapped to the cow's head, between the ears, with wires leading down to the glass eyes, both of which rolled incessantly to an electronic pulse.

Brandon scowled at Penny. "You're late, darling."

"Sorry, the performance piece went on, and on. You know how it is. I don't recognize the cameraman, Brandie—you know how strangers bother me."

"Can't be helped. Ellis is down with meningitis. Meet Scott."

"Do I have to?" Penny whined, then, offering a bright smile at Scott, who stood bemusedly behind the camera, she waved and said, "Wonderful to meet you, Scott. Shall we begin taping?"

"Anytime," Scott said, shrugging.

Penny gave her husband a nod; Brandon gave Scott a nod. Scott glanced over at Penny, who nodded, then at Max, who nodded. "Okay," Scott said, "we're rolling."

"Wait!" Brandon called out. "I want to change the order! Where's our guest?"

Penny rolled her eyes. "Not due for another ten minutes, darling. Let's stick with the script, please?"

"Oh, all right. Okay, I'm ready. Everyone ready?"

Everyone nodded.

Brandon faced the camera, composed himself, then smiled and said in his deep rolling voice, "Welcome, friends, once again to Northern Order

Magazine's program on the arts, coming to you this week from the Art Place Gallery at Outré Space in the heart of this vibrant, wonderful city." He paused, took a step closer to the cow. "Today, we'll look into the seminal centrepiece of Johan Guppy's ground-breaking, innovative show, *A Cow's-eye View*, which has been on display here for the past twenty-six months, to much acclaim." He strode to the cow's side and laid a hand on its back. "This piece, entitled *Cow*, is a wonderful example of interactive art. The intent, for the viewer, is obvious." He walked around to the back of the cow, then faced the camera again. "One must proceed, through the installation, until one's eye comes into contact with the camera's eyepiece." Brandon rolled up the sleeves of his casual cardigan, revealing his broad, hairy wrists—which, Max guessed, were Brandon's own personal favourite features. "Art always makes demands of its audience, and *Cow* is no exception." He smiled once again and Scott nodded, indicating he was zooming in, then Brandon turned to the cow's anus and pushed his head against it. "No doubt," he grunted, pushing steadily, "It's a tight squeeze. If you'll be patient."

Max stared in amazement as Brandon exerted his prodigious strength and managed to push his entire head up the cow's anus. He continued speaking, but of course the words were too muffled to understand. And Brandon kept on pushing. Max glanced over at Penny, who stood with one index finger pressed to her surgically amassed lips, a quizzical frown rippling her brow. Then he glanced over at Scott, whose mouth was hanging open, his eyes glazed, drool dripping down onto the camera's swing-grip. Brandon was now gesticulating, his voice rising in timbre.

"Uh, darling," Penny said, "I'm not sure—"

Brandon's arms began waving, then pushing then beating at the cow's hips. The cow rocked on its stand. Brandon was now yelling.

Penny whirled to Max and Scott. "Well, for godsakes, help him!"

Both men ran forward.

Ten minutes later, Brandon, his face blotched red and hair dotted with stuffing, sat swivelling on an easy chair, watching as his guest took her seat opposite him. He smiled. "I understand, Lucy, you will be gracing this moment with a reading, selected from your most recent collection of poetry." He smiled at the camera, "This collection, entitled *Mommy*

Mommy Mommy, a collection of poems for and about Mommies, is now available at choice outlets. Ladies and gentlemen, Lucy Mort will now read from her new work."

Lucy—who to Max looked smaller than the last time he'd seen her, which, he recalled, was that dreadful night at Culture Quo—glanced up at the camera lense, offered a tight, shaky smile, then bent her gaze to the page on her lap. She took a deep breath, then, her voice thin and vibrating, she read,

Mum, mum mum-mum
jam in the cupboard, yum
Saturday mornings in the sun
cream and flatbread under thumb
and this is why, mum-yum,
I dreamed of locking you
in there—the cupboard.

She rattled the page, then sat back and smiled over at Brandon, who nodded with an expression of thoughtful appreciation. "Excellent, Lucy, well done. I understand that the collection has been reviewed extensively in the past month or so, since the book was launched."

Scott scrambled at the manual focus, and Max blinked uncertainly as, for the briefest of moments, it seemed that, upon receipt of Brandon's words, Lucy Mort's head shrunk, ever so slightly.

"Well," she snapped. "What do they know? Critics are scum of the earth. They said the essays read like a thesis! Can you imagine that? The selection committee loved it! They hate women, even the women critics, they hate women, it's as plain as that. All my friends loved it—some even paid for their own copy! I don't have to take this, I'm not here to be criticized. No one has the right to criticize my work—it's poetry! It's personal! I'm very hurt!"

"Dear Lucy," Brandon soothed, leaning close. "Lucy dear, dear Lucy, you well know my opinions on those critics who see nothing but negativity in everything they review. As you recall, my own review of *Mommy Mommy Mommy* was effusive in its praise—as I always am, no matter what you write."

"No matter what I write? What's that supposed to mean?"

Scott snatched at the manual focus again, and to Max, Lucy's shoulders seemed huge below the poet's head.

"Only, Lucy dear, that whatever you write is simply brilliant, as far as I'm concerned, and," he added with a smile to the camera, "who is this city's premiere guru of the art scene? Upon whom does this entire city depend for their wise, cultured opinions on art and culture? I need not answer that immodestly, need I?"

"Of course you're right," Lucy said, sighing. "Thank you. I love you, Brandon. We all love you. We love you even more than we do your more famous brother, Brendan—it's true, for all of us—"

Scott whimpered as he readjusted the focus on Brandon's head, which had just gotten larger and was turning bright red, the old red blotches turning white at the same time. Brandon leaned dangerously close to Lucy, who shrank back in alarm. "My brother?" he rasped. *"My brother?* How dare you mention his name to me—"

"Hey!" Scott shouted. "I thought you *were* your brother! Oh! Sorry! I'm so sorry, I didn't realize—"

"Shut up!" Brandon roared, surging to his feet.

"Cut!" Penny screamed. "Cut! Cut! Cut!" She rushed forward to soothe her husband, whose veins were pulsing madly on his thick neck and against his temples. "We'll do an edit job! We'll edit it right! Everyone calm down!"

Lucy was crying. "I'm sorry, Brandon! I'm so sorry!"

Max saw his moment, and stepped forward. "Excuse me, Mr Safeword," he said quietly, drawing everyone's attention. Into the dangerous silence, Max said, "I've heard of you, of course. But I didn't know you had a brother. Brendan, is it? I've never heard of him. Is he someone important? You know, I think I'd have heard of him if he was someone important, don't you think?"

Brandon stared at Max for a long, tense moment, then his broad smile split his robust features. "You must be the new boy! Welcome aboard!"

5. *Homo vegetabilis*

Sool Koobie tracked the tweed-clad professor from Culture Quo, staying always a half dozen silent steps behind the man as he wandered the dark, ill-lit streets of the city's core. Don Palmister paused every few moments, his neck straining as he looked up at one dilapidated building after another. He mumbled under his breath and occasionally pulled out a small notepad and jotted down details, then resumed his peregrination.

This time, Sool Koobie knew, this one wouldn't get away from him. The last time had been a real mess. He'd thought his target to be a girl, and after piercing its belly and dragging the flopping body away from the rest of the small herd, he'd begun the task of dressing down the carcass in a dark alley. Although the victim was still alive, twitching and moaning, Sool immediately set his chert knife to its chest. Upon cutting away the select morsels that were the breasts, Sool found in his hands two blood-smeared bags of liquid. At that moment the victim screamed and rolled to its feet. Sool was a moment too late in pursuing, as the creature emerged onto the street and nearly ran into a passing car, which screeched to a halt, and the hunt was up for Sool Koobie.

Tonight, driven by hunger, Sool chose not to wait in ambush, but to stalk his quarry, and tonight, he'd make sure of things.

A wind was blowing, whining along the alleys and streets. Restaurants were closing up as the hour was late, and Don Palmister was alone, unmindful, and as far as Sool could discern, unarmed. The smell of various vegetables emanating from the man left an olfactory trail that made Sool's mouth water. He closed a step behind the man.

He'd made the proper propitiations, and the stars were kind in their glittering alignment overhead, the spirits at peace, the Mother casting down a benign eye on the natural process of things, to which Sool was intricately attuned. He'd danced the cycle of life and death, and a soothing calm had come over him, making him a part of all things, and each thing, and the thing to come.

As the quarry paused at the mouth of an alley and pulled out its notepad and pen, Sool Koobie leapt forward. The neanderthal caught the professor entirely unawares, driving his spear into the man's back hard enough to plunge its stone tip out through the chest. The professor grunted softly, then sagged, his notepad and pen falling to the pavement. Sool paused over the body and crowed silently at the night sky, then he grabbed the body's ankles and quickly pulled it into the alley. A moment later he had the deadweight on one shoulder. Spear in hand, Sool Koobie jogged through the darkness. He would dress the kill far away—out beyond the city's edges, where grass and trees and abandoned buildings would provide him certain privacy.

In Sool Koobie's chest, his heart danced happily. He felt noble in his savagery, right down to the grime-rimmed curved nails on his wide, crooked toes.

6. The late-night hate session

Minister of Art and Culture Paul Silverthump stood at the window of his office, looking down, with hands clasped behind him, at the city below. "No," he said, "even lower than scum. Less than bacteria, more inisidious than viruses, smellier than the crap stuck on my underwear after a minutes briefing. And what's worse, there's more and more of them, everyday there's more. They should all be shot, crushed underfoot, ground into the grit and dust of their miserable hovels. I'm a believer in survival of the fittest, Andy, you know that. Me and my kind, we know what it's all about. I'm petitioning in my neighbourhood for a high wall, Andy, the highest in the city. And private security guards. We'll keep them out, remove them from our sight, destroy them with our contempt and ministerial indifference. We're getting fewer, that's the problem, the imbalance is getting problematic, no doubt about it. We need to start systematically culling numbers: make a list, Andy. There's measures to continue: starvation, though that's slow; institutionally-encouraged suicide through bureaucratic immobility— that's the other ministry's sphere of activity, of course, and let's face it, our SS boys and girls are doing a damned fine job, especially having added indirect support of substance abuse, malnutrition, bad education, and media-backed indifference. It's good, Andy, what they're doing is good work. We need to learn from them, we need to emulate their methods." He paused. A pigeon slammed against the windowpane in front of him, but Paul didn't even flinch. "Look at them down there—not that I can actually see them—who'd want to. The commonry. People. Suffering, miserable, deprived, poor, disadvantaged, disenfranchized, ineffectual people. The citizens, God I hate them."

He went on, but tonight Andy "Kit" Breech's mind was on other things. He'd lost another nonstaring contest with Kit earlier that evening, after Lucy had left and he'd changed the sheets. Kit's refusal to meet his gaze was all the proof Andy needed to confirm that something serious was going on, and that, added to what he'd discovered in the dresser drawer in his bedroom, was more than enough to leave Andy . . . *scared. That's what I am. Damned scared. Someone rummaged through my box of condoms, someone leaving slime in his wake. Who could that be, I wonder? And it's a big box, five thousand condoms, each slick with slime, as if Kit had been . . . counting them. Why count them? What's he up to? What is it about my condoms? What do I do now? Where do I go from here? Take a memo. Asap. My god we're in trouble aren't we. Research the problem, pronto. I want contingency plans, I want scenarios, and I want them yesterday, dammit. Go to the library, go to the university, go to the fisheries branch, pet shops, diving enthusiasts, ministers, teachers, nuns—I don't care who, but find for me the answers I need. What's he thinking? What's he planning? What's he keep looking at out the balcony window? What's in that closet? How did he pick all those new locks? And why was he examining, one by one, five thousand condoms? I need to know these things, before it's too late, before I lose my mind. Asap, hop to it, pronto . . .*

"There's no hell more frightening than the world down there," Paul Silverthump was saying. "Normal people, my God, the sheer filth of their existence makes me want to throw up my veal cordon bleu, hah, that'll give those damn pigeons something to munch on. Have you instructed the exterminator, Andy?"

"Hmm? Oh, yes of course, Paul. He says it's highly unlikely you are being individually pursued by the city's pigeons—"

"I don't care what the bastard says. I know what I know, Andy.

They're after me. I can't step outside anymore. They kamikaze my windows, here and at home. In the car, in restaurants, in bars, in meetings. They chase me around, Andy. I want the city's pigeons dead, all of them, and I want it done now, this instant."

"Of course, Paul. I'll make another call."

"Malathion," Paul said. "We'll call it anticipatory spraying for mosquitoes. But I want pigeon-lethal concentrations—"

"Might prove human-lethal, Paul—"

"I don't give a shit. Let them all drop like flies. We're better off without all of them. Give us important figures gas masks or something, or open up those nuclear shelters down below—we can wait it out, no problem, and hey, only the fittest of the fittest will emerge from those shelters come the dawn. You and me, Andy, we'll be on top, and that's how it should be."

"On top of what, Sir?"

"Don't give me that shit, Andy. I know your soul. You sold it to me years ago. I know your contempt, that icy chunk of nadir you call a heart, pumping to the blood let by others, so shove the smarmy remarks, Andy. One snap of my fingers and you'll be pigeon feed— before they all kick off, of course."

Andy smiled blandly at the Minister. *Asshole, that's what you think. I've outlived every minister in this fucking office, and I'll outlive you and your miniscule career, Paul. Count on it. You stumble, like all your kind, but I slide. You've got your tricks, your evasions, your denials, your bald-faced braving it out with lawyers point, flank and taking up the rear. If you're still clean, Paul, it's because I've kept you that way. And I've got the secret files to prove it, so don't fuck with me, Paul. Never fuck with me. Who the hell do you think trained all those pigeons?*

"Get outa here," Paul growled, turning back to the window. "Call that exterminator, set up the malathion program—"

"Could be difficult, Paul."

"Why?"

"Well, why would the Ministry of Art and Culture issue a bug-spraying directive?"

"Find me an answer, Andy. That's your job. Now, stop wasting my fucking time."

Andy kept his smile as he rose to his feet. "I'm on it. Goodnight, Paul. Oh, by the way, the copter and limo and bodyguards have been arranged for the Awards Night."

"Good," Paul grunted. "Make sure those guards are armed to the teeth, Andy. Someone might want to . . . touch me."

Just the pigeons, Paul. "See you tomorrow, then." He headed out, leaving the minister alone with his rabid thoughts.

Not that he's exceptional in his beliefs. Just look at the bloody premier. But you're all making a mistake, fellas. That mob out there is getting all too hungry, all too pissed off with every fucking one of you. When they move, it'll be to take off your heads and stick em on spears. And that'll leave people like me, in the know, capable, sympathetic and righteous, victims of policy just like everyone else. We'll put things in order, and the beast's ugly head will subside once again into its comatose, vegetative state, and you and your cronies, Paul, will be fertilizer.

I could give Kit away. To the zoo or something. But I have to act quickly. Before he makes his move, whatever that is. Asap. Pronto.

PART THREE

The Fruitful Church of Disobedience

1. Thursday's Lounge

Seeking comfort, and more than a little concerned about his burgeoning
appearance, Arthur Revell sought the companionship of his few friends,
who would at this time of night be found in the establishment called
Chesterton's, in the lounge next to the restaurant, known as Thursday's.

Arthur's friends numbered two. One was the owner of the place, Tobias Laugh, and the other was a successful painter of landscapes and
wildlife, Elana Oxbow. He found them at a table near the kitchen entrance, at the very back of Thursday's. The other patrons in the lounge
seemed to collectively recoil as Arthur walked past, leading him to scowl
desultorily. It had been a miserable night already, and things just seemed
to be getting worse and worse. He arrived at the table and, ignoring the
stunned expressions on Toby's and Elana's faces, he pulled back the
small chair and levered his massive frame into it. The chair creaked
warningly as he settled in.

"Good lord, Arthur," Tobias said, "what's happened?"

"I went on a date, with a lovely woman named Faye. We'd just sat
down to eat and she'd just asked me what I do for a living, to which I
intended to reply that I'm a part-time professional specializing in part-
time employment in various sectors in the service, maintenance and other
such industries, when I felt this indescribable pain." He pointed to the
two knobby horns that now jutted from above his brow ridges, one to
either side of his forehead. "Here, and here. And my teeth started hurting
terribly, and the arms of the chair broke simultaneously, then the legs,
and I could feel how much denser I'd suddenly become, and how much
bigger. Poor Faye, she screamed, then fled. What could I do? What could
I say? It was horrible, far worse than, say, finding a pimple an hour before the date, you know, the kind that gets redder and redder and then the

108

white pustule rises like a volcano, and you know if you pop it, you'll have to squeeze all that stuff out, and then it'll bleed, and the red mark will get even bigger. So you put some kind of disguising cream on it, but it dries and cracks and you end up flaking into your soup, and the blood flows all over again, and you see how she's looking and looking at it and then, when she sees you watching, she tries to look away, to look everywhere but at the massive wound on your face, but she can't, not really, and that's the last time you ever go out with her."

"Actually," Elana said, eyeing him carefully, "there's some spirits that look much like what you seem to be becoming— I know an old shaman—"

"No no," Arthur shook his head. "That won't be necessary. I phoned Dr Payne—my gastrointestinologist—and he confirmed that there might be side effects to the medication I'm taking for my infection. He was kind enough to send me a secondary treatment, by courier." Arthur reached into his shirt pocket and pulled out a second pill bottle. "I don't know what it is, but I do feel better. The horns have stopped moving, anyway."

"Moving?" Tobias asked, running a hand through his wild white mane of hair. "They were moving? How?"

"Well, waving about, I suppose. Reacting to, uh, sounds, I think, like a dog's ears."

"So," Tobias said. "Not horns at all, but antennae. Let's see those pills."

Arthur handed the bottle to his old friend.

"125 mg," Tobias read, "Malathion. Now, why does that word ring a bell? Elana?"

"Beats me. Do you mind if I touch them, Arthur?"

"No, I suppose not."

The young woman reached up and probed the projections. "Can you feel this?"

"Oh, yes."

"Well, they feel like horns to me. Wouldn't there be some kind of tympanic membrane, Toby? Some kind of obvious sensory apparatus?"

"You have a point there," Tobias admitted. "So you're being treated for your ulcer?"

Arthur shook his head. "I do not possess an ulcer, but an infection. It may be endemic, in that I am physically responding to the country's economic ills, making me susceptible to takeover bids."

"Did your doctor suggest this?" Tobias asked.

"He expressed his concern. The insurance industry is not doing well, after all. I've since given the situation more thought. Clearly I'm unwell. Now, as the newspapers point out, the country is also unwell. I feel poorly, and the poor are on the increase, even given the constant changing of the poverty level by the federal statisticians. My needs are not being met in innumerable contexts—for example, I'm still a virgin, I can't hold my liquor as much as I might want to; I can't smoke cigarettes because it makes my cheeks swell, and I would surely love to indulge the habit; illicit drugs would interfere with my medication, not to mention my sense of reality. I'm not being socially served. Now, the coincidences continue. I'm getting hungrier, sicker, heavier, less inclined to physical motion, with an unquenchable taste for bad American television programs and infomercials. I'm also complacent, occasionally smug, with a growing coldness in my heart that is expressed in a lack of sympathy for my lesser fellows. If I had a dog, I believe I would feed it before I fed a homeless waif in an alleyway, then I'd kick the dog. Does this make sense? Without question, my friends, I believe I am a direct causal consequence of the pervasive collective misalignment of our nation's citizens with the natural exigencies of survival in the modern world. And if this is not sufficiently disturbing, I now have horns, weigh four hundred pounds without much increase in actual mass, and am four inches taller than I was this morning. The country needs saving, my friends, if only to purge me of my personal discomfort."

"Dear me," Elana said, genuine concern in her expression, "I can't imagine you being cold hearted about anything, Arthur."

"No, it's true," he protested. "I don't care anymore. I don't care about children, pets, disabled people, gays, lesbians, racial minorities, linguistically challenged people, juvenile delinquency, drugs, alcohol abuse, child abuse, spousal abuse, smokers, farters, nose-pickers, heart disease, radioactive waste, Native self-government, poor people, fat people, tainted blood, historical oppression, terrorism, the RCMP, the Jets, the Leafs, Hillary's fingerprints, insane cattle, endangered whales, the fur industry, baby seals, illiteracy, separatism, multiculturalism, technophiles, the Net, porcelain hedgehogs, cynicism, nihilism, and antiestablishmentarianism. In fact, I care about only one thing: money. I don't have any. Why not? That's what I care about, and I swear, once I've got it, I'm going to hold onto it, even if the whole world ends up in flames and ruin. Dammit."

"So," Tobias said, "what makes you so different?"

Arthur stared at the old man. "You mean . . . "

"Exactly," Tobias said. "You should run for office. Any office. The Big Office, in fact. You'll win."

"But I would let everything dissolve into a chaotic quagmire through my cynical contempt and my affected indifference, and my insulated perceptions would ensure the social collapse of anyone remotely unlike me."

"Right."

"But that's inhuman, Tobias!"

The old man smiled. "Bingo. And that, Arthur dear, is why you do not suffer from the country's ills. If you've come to reflect its ills, as it seems you have, then you must find an outlet—you must learn a means of reflecting back what is cast upon you. What else can you do?"

"I don't know. What's happening to me?"

"Self-discovery, I'd guess. Wait and see."

"Is it safe?"

"Beats me. You trust this Dr Payne?"

"I think so. He seems very busy, very much involved with work of paramount, and secretive, importance. In fact, he is constantly in communication with the entymology department at the hospital. It seems they require his assistance continually. I'm very impressed."

"Entymology?" Elana asked.

"Yes. Containment Room B."

"Will you be seeing him again?" she asked, frowning slightly.

"Well, not for some time," Arthur said. "I have two refills on both prescriptions, after all. Oh, and Faye told me he's been sent away, possibly for some time. Why do you ask?''

"<u>Curious</u>, that's all.''

"Malathion's a pesticide!'' Tobias exclaimed, snatching the bottle from Arthur's hands. "Stop taking this, Arthur! My God, you could've poisoned yourself! Killed yourself! Someone's made a terrible mistake!''

"But I need those,'' Arthur pleaded, pointing at his horns. "What if they get bigger?''

"Taking malathion's not going to change that, son,'' Tobias said, looking shaken. "Trust me, please.''

Arthur hesitated, then sighed. "Of course I trust you, Tobias. You're a good friend. All right, you can keep the pills.''

"Arthur,'' Elana said, "have you seen John Gully around lately?''

"No, I don't think so. He's that dropped-out architect, isn't he?''

"Yes. I think he might be in trouble, him and his colony. If you see him, let him know someone's hunting him. Someone from the railroad.''

"Sure, Elana.''

"Cheer up, Arthur,'' Tobias said, "I'll buy you a big glass of milk.''

Arthur's expression assumed an uncharacteristic, nasty eagerness. "Milk?'' he snarled. "The hell with milk, buster, give me a Jack Daniels, doubled up, no ice, no water!'' After a moment his face cleared and he blinked bemusedly at his staring friends. "Something wrong?'' he asked quietly.

"Uhm,'' Tobias said, "no, Arthur, I don't think so.''

"Gimme a smoke, Elana,'' Arthur growled, scratching the bristle on his chin. "I ain't had a nail in hours!''

"My god,'' Elana said to Tobias. "He's *changing*.''

"You're right,'' Tobias breathed. "But into what?''

2. The Sanger Sock

It was an hour past midnight. Wearing his combat fatigues, Joey "Rip" Sanger shoulder-rolled across the tracks and slid down the gravel embankment into the high grasses in the ditch. He pulled down his IR goggles and scanned the countryside. Two of his beepers had chirped, less than ten minutes back, just down the spur's line. Ahead rose a leaning silo, a slightly glowing blotch through his goggles, the old wood still bleeding the day's heat. Summer came fast in the prairies—just two days ago it had snowed, and now everything was turning green under a blistering sun. Joey felt sweat trickle the length of his scar.

There was someone in the darkness up ahead. Maybe a runner, maybe a scout. Joey planned to take him down, apply some squeeze, and get a guide right back to the squatter's camp. He tightened the straps on his leather gloves, then hitched himself into a squat, paused a moment, then slipped forward.

The last thing he expected to stumble on, in the silo's inky shadows, was a scattering of split, bloody, flesh-streaked bones. His goggles showed them warmer than the ground they laid on, and then he found a blood-stained, ripped-up tweed jacket, carelessly half-buried in gravel. Joey hesitated. This wasn't right. This was nasty, plain nasty. Still, he'd handled nasty before. If the damned squatters were cannibals, well, he'd seen worse. At least, he felt sure he had, somewhere.

A scuffling noise directly ahead alerted him to a nearby presence. Joey tensed himself, flexing his hands, getting ready for the Sanger Sock— he'd need it tonight, he was now certain. These squatters weren't pushovers, nosiree. They were mean, they were prairie boys down to their ugly, rock-hard, bloodthirsty core. Well, they were about to meet Joey "Rip" Sanger from Scarborough.

A twig snapped behind him and, swearing, Joey whirled. Crouched in front of him was a naked, hairy man, his teeth bared and his eyes gleaming in the moonlight.

"A Luddite!" Joey hissed.

"Arlubye!" the man hissed back.

"Your time's up, bastard!"

"Yortimssup, basarr!"

"Come along peacibly, fella."

"Guhmlahnbeesly, bela."

Joey's eyes narrowed. "You mocking my Ontario accent? Fine, have it that way. Ever heard of the Sanger Sock? You're about to make its acquaintance, y'poor sod."

"Yablah," the man said.

Joey jumped the man, his fists whistling a blinding flurry of blows.

The moon had almost set when Joey woke up, feeling like death run over by Donald the Deisel Engine. There wasn't a single area of his body that didn't feel bruised, not a bone that didn't feel broken, not a hair left that wasn't crinkled and split at the ends. "What happened?" he mumbled.

A clear, calm voice answered. "Not sure, friend. Lucky we came on you when we did. Someone out there doesn't like you. Had you spreadeagled on the tracks. Lucky for you I keep a point, or we'd have rolled right over you. Jojum damn near stepped on you as it was."

Blinking blearily, Joey tried to sit up, was surprised that he could, and looked around. He sighed. "By God, it really is a 57 Wells, isn't it? Mint condition, too." He saw the man who'd been speaking—dishevelled but somehow clean looking, thinning gray hair, a lean, strong frame, a face of solidly prescribed angles and planes, and eyes that were sharp with intelligence. "Who the hell are you?" Joey rasped.

The man smiled. "The one you're looking for, Mr Sanger. The name's John Gully. You're riding on Gully's Block, as the boys and girls like to call it. Ergonomically designed, a shanty town on wheels, fully self-sufficient, with a hydroponics car, a freeze car stocked with meat purchased from local ranchers, and modestly luxurious accommodations to suit three hundred people. We stay out of everyone's way, we provide a safehouse for the homeless of the city, we rehabilitate, teach trades, run our own justice system, use our own currency—gold, in fact."

"How in hell you afford all that, bud?"

Gully smiled. "I was an architect, once, from a wealthy family. I inherited, invested, made bundles, then dropped out."

"And that's it? You're some kind of eccentric patron of the poor? Geez, what a sorry story."

The man shrugged. "Not really. I just wanted out. Plain and simple, but the creative impulses remained. I needed a challenge. I found one."

"Well," Joey struggled to his feet, groaning softly before taking a deep breath. "The challenge is over, Gully. I'm shutting you down."

"I was afraid of that. And here I thought you, more than anyone else,

114

would appreciate what I've done here."

"Why in hell should I do that?"

"The history, the tradition. This city was built on the rails. No one cares anymore, and it's all going down the tubes. Faded glory. What a waste. We've gotten so scared of taking risks, we'll just letting ourselves sink into mediocre oblivion. It's a damned shame, if you ask me. The people running your life, Mr Sanger, they have no hearts, no sense of wonder, no ambition beyond self-serving greed; and they don't give a damn about you, so long as you do jobs for them. When it comes time for you to retire, they'll expect you to just drift away, find some hovel, cash your measly pension cheques, vote conservative, and grumble about the youth of the day and live in terror of those who have not, but want. And they'll keep smiling and reassuring and feeding your paranoia until you're dropped six feet down and rotting in a pine box."

"Not Joey "Rip" Sanger, they won't."

John Gully laughed. "You're a lifer, Mr Sanger. A product of inertia, collective malaise. Single-minded, stubborn, your own man—sure, all those things to comfort your sense of self-worth, but it's all an illusion because when it's all said and done, you toe the line just like the rest of them."

"Heard about enough of your sermon, preacher. Lay on the steam and let's roll 'er into the yards. I'm beat and my ears ache."

"Sorry, can't do that, Mr Sanger."

With these words three large men entered the engine room, carrying ropes. Jocy groaned a second time. There wasn't enough left in him to resist. He glared at John Gully as the men tied him up. "Plan to dump me off a tressle?"

"Tressle? As in tressle bridge?" John laughed. "We're on the prairie, remember? There aren't any tressles. No, we'll just hold on to you till things blow over—"

"I won't blow over," Joey said. "You'll have to kill me."

"Why bother saving you, then? Oh no, we're not murderers. We'll think of something, I'm sure. In the meantime, relax, Mr Sanger. You've got some healing up to do. Who took you out, by the way?"

"A cannibal Luddite, I think. With a speech impediment."

"Ahh, so you've met Sool Koobie, then."

"Who?"

"A neanderthal. It's a long story, but consider yourself lucky. He must've been well fed; either that or you eat meat three times a day—"

"Damn right I do," Joey growled. "I ain't no sussy."

"Lucky you."

Joey fell silent. At the moment, he felt anything but lucky. His Sanger Sock had failed. For the first time in generations, it had failed. He was a broken man, and the feeling was new to him, and he didn't like it one bit.

3. The table invites

The Habby Modeler's owner stood uncertainly behind the counter, surrounded by glass-fronted cases containing his military and science-fiction model collection. He had one hand behind his back, and his t-shirt was greyish white with the words "SMALL IS BETTER" emblazoned on it. The man peered at Max through thick glasses, craning his neck and shifting whenever Max edged down one of the rows and out of sight.

Sweat ran down Max's body, cool under the satin shirt he was wearing. He clutched a folded page of instructions in one damp hand. *Habby. What an idiot. Happy, hobby, yeah, right. Cute as cow pies, fella. Shit, I'm running out of time.* He checked his watch. He was due at the table at Culture Quo in ten minutes, and then, immediately following supper, they'd all trek off to the annual Awards Night at the Unified Cultural Workers Assembly Hall—otherwise known to city denizens as "the Pyramid." And then he'd receive his award as Most Promising Artist of the Year, and a cheque for ten grand.

Hissing in frustration under his breath, Max headed towards the counter, and the sloppy, overweight man behind it. "Technical question," Max said, smiling.

"Only kind I can answer," the man replied. "How many King Tigers did Nazi Germany issue in 1944? I know. How close was the V-3 rocket to full-scale production? I know. What size were Patton's army boots? I know. To what extent did Hegel's philosophy influence Adolf's private gardener. I—"

"Yeah, I know," Max cut in. "You know. But tell me this." He unfolded the instructions and laid it out on the counter.

"Ooh," the man said, "Special Edition Klingon battle cruiser—you musta bought that years ago—"

"Yeah yeah, listen. Look here, the instructions says part 6B attaches to part 7A."

"Yeah, so?"

"So, there is no 6B! There's a 6A, and a 7B, but no 6B! How the hell can I complete my sculpture without 6B!"

"Sculpture? That's a model."

"Shut the fuck up. You're talking to an artist here, not some creepy weasel-faced chip-stuffed pimple factory."

"Yeah, right," the man drawled. "Well, did you look in the box? Coulda come loose from the plastic trees."

"Of course I looked. It's not there."

"Huh. Well, sometimes the company screws up. Sometimes a part gets left out. That makes your kit a collector's item—something wrong?"

Max stared at the man blankly. "Left out?"

"Yeah, sure. Happens all the time. You just have to send for the part. Or, hell, I'll swap you with one of the newer models—they look neater, anyway. Those guys—" he pointed at the carboard box, "don't even know the cruiser's real name."

"How can they leave a part out? What the hell am I going to do? I need a sculpture right now, in the next five minutes." Max's gaze cast wildly around the store, fixed at last on the finished models behind the man.

Scowling, the man said, "I don't sell my World War II stuff, and even if I did, it'd be damned expensive."

"I can pay it. Give me that tank—"

"Like hell I will. That's a Swedish S-tank. Piece of garbage on the battlefield, but it's a collector's item."

"I'll pay anything."

"Not the S-tank." The man still had one hand behind his back, and seemed to be working at something there.

"Well, what do you have that you'll sell?"

"Assembled? Well, I got two copies of the submarine from that old TV series in the sixties. Remember *Voyage to the Bottom of the Sea?*"

"Imaginative title," Max snapped. "Let's see the damned thing."

"Well, the one I'd sell has had some, uh, improvements on it. I did it when I was a kid, you see. Not even a serious collector yet, you understand—"

"Let's see it!"

The man reached with his free hand under the counter and pulled out a long plastic submarine, its nose dish shaped. On its underside were four wheels. "I stuck a motor in it," the man explained. "Nickel-Cadmium batteries, probably still runs. Let's check—"

"I don't care if it runs, you asshole. How much?"

"With an attitude like yours, *asshole,* two hundred bucks, firm."

Max pulled out his wallet and tossed down one of his many credit cards. "Fine."

"We don't take credit cards," the man smirked. "Cash. No cheques, either. Cash."

"Scumbag, I'm a Nacht—recognise the name?"

"No."

"The Nachts are in lingerie. Filthy rich."

"Yeah, well, I'm outa that phase. I still want cash."

"Fine!" Max pulled out a wad of bills. "You just fucked up my supper, prick." He counted out ten twenties, slapped them on the table, then had to wait while the man counted them again, all with one hand. "Got a gun back there or something?" Max asked.

"I wish. Sometimes my anus closes right up. I gotta work it loose again, or everything backs up, if you know what I mean. You want me to wrap it?"

"Uh, no. A box will do."

"Yeah but there's some highly breakable protuberances—"

"Do I give a shit? I paid for it. It's mine. I can do what the hell I want with it. Now hand it over."

The man had found a long flower box, but he now draped his arm protectively over it, his eyes wide, dribbles of sweat running down from his greasy hair. "I made it," he whined. "You're not supposed to break it."

"Just a joke, friend," Max said, smiling. "Honest. I'll take good care of it. Now can I have it please? I've got a dinner date with a table."

"You're dating a table? Cool." The man pushed the box towards Max, who snatched it up. "Hey!" the man shouted as Max rushed to the door, "I'm loosening up!"

Six minutes later Max reached the door of Culture Quo. The restaurant was packed with pre-Awards patrons, and the air was humming with feigned excitement. Max pushed through the lineup, jabbing recalcitrant s.o.b.'s with the flower box until he stepped clear.

And there it was. The table. Where he'd dreamed of sitting, there in the company of greatness or, at the very least, self-importance. And the empty chair—two of them in fact—and Brandon Safeword gesticulating as he pontificated to his adoring audience consisting of his wife, Penny Foote-Safeword, and Lucy Mort. Max blinked uncertainly as he approached. Brandon's head looked too big, and Lucy's too small, as if someone had been messing with the camera lense through which Max observed—not that he was observing these details through a camera lense. Even so, what met his eyes seemed strangely skewed.

"Ahh, Maximillian!" Brandon called out. Many heads turned, the conversations at the other tables stilling for a brief moment as eyes fixed on Max, who arrived at the table and pulled out a chair and then sat down. "Excellent timing, my boy," Brandon said. "We were just about to order."

Penny thrust a menu into Max's hand. He set down the flower box, edged it with a foot under his own chair, then turned his attention to the menu:

Culture Quo

organic vegetarian dining

appetisers

barley soup
thirty-six grain toast
feral garden salad

barley water
barley tea
wheat milk
soya milk

main courses

triticale quiche (sans eggs)
soya prime rib
scampi-shell salad
precious porridge
wheat stirfry (with ginger)
bannock (made with canola oil)

on the side

brown rice plain
soya rice plain
wild rice plain
birch bark plain

desserts

oat cakes
soya-shell apple pie
yeast-free canola cookies
sugar-free ice-water (the fluffy slushy)

alcoholic drinks

lite draft
lite ale
lite red wine
lite white wine
lite citrus coolers
lite alcohol plain

Lucy's voice came out as a tiny squeak. "I'll have the feral garden salad, wheat stirfry with birch bark plain on the side, and a double lite-alcohol. Thanks."

Smacking her lips, Penny said, "Were the scampi harvested in dolphin-safe nets? Excellent. I'll have that, and brown rice plain. No, no appetiser— I'd be stuffed! And a triple lite alcohol plain. Marvelous. Brandon darling?"

"Oh no, Maximillian first, by all means."

"Uh, thanks. I'll have the thirty-six grain toast, the triticale quiche, and a lite ale, please."

"Sounds perfect," Brandon said to Max. "Of course," he added, leaning over to nudge Max with an iron-hard forearm, "as Emcee tonight, the last thing I'd need is all that roughage ringing the old bell below, eh? Hah hah! Ho ho! No, instead, I'll have the soya prime rib, with wild rice, and wheat milk to preserve my elocution. Wonderful, we're all set!"

"Where's Professor Palmister?" Max asked.

"Vanished," Brandon intoned. "A cause for great concern. Left not a trace of his whereabouts, and believe me, it's not like him to miss this of all nights. Nine out of the ten incipient award-winners come from his class, after all."

Max glanced at Lucy, who taught at the rival university. Her miniscule face was bent down towards the glass of mineral water in her hands.

"Next year, of course," Brandon drawled, "the balance will shift, right Lucy?"

She nodded mutely, not looking up. The purse on her lap was inordinately large, long, bulky, and she reached down with one hand to stroke it a couple times, then reached back up to her glass.

The appetisers arrived. Max had hoped to add to the conversation somewhat, but the thirty-six grain toast swelled into a glutinous, doughy ball in his mouth, and he was left chewing on his first bite until the main courses arrived. In the meantime, Brandon spoke, "Ever been to the Pyramid, Max? Thought not. A wonderful work of art in itself, housing the city's finest publicly-owned collection of fine art. Well, publicly-owned is something of a misnomer, we'd all not hesitate to admit—at least in private, hah hah! The galleries are sealed against pollution, and that includes uninvited people across the board, and the wonder of it is, the Board of Directors ensure that few—very few indeed—are ever invited to peruse the collection. I, of course, have been many times. Truly remarkable. Brilliant work, all of it, packed chock-full with seminal meanings, dire significance, cultural value. There's even a copy of Penny's book, stored in an airtight, alarm-fitted cabinet, in a room all its own."

The main courses arrived. Max managed to swallow down the mouthful of toast and, greatly relieved, permitted the waitress to remove the rest. "Is the collection very large?" he asked. "I've seen the building from the outside. It's huge."

"There are seven works of art in the Pyramid," Brandon said. "Each a treasure in its own right. Most of the lottery funding went into constructing the edifice, naturally, and these days into the salaries of the two hundred staff members. A triumph of city planning, the envy of cities the world over."

There followed five minutes of nonverbal utterances as everyone tucked into their suppers: crunching, slurping, gnawing, nibbling, chewing— mostly chewing, although the loudest sound assailing Max's ears was the twin cavernous whistles issuing from Brandon's enormous nostrils. His head appeared to have grown larger since Max first sat down, and each breath Brandon drew in seemed to create a momentary vacuum in the centre of the table, followed by a hair-flicking gust. No one else seemed to notice, even though Lucy's head was pulled and pushed with alarming force, giving her trouble in matching her forkfuls of food with her mouth.

Desserts were then ordered, and when the plates were scraped clean, Brandon leaned back with a loud atmospherically traumatizing sigh and said, "We'd best be off, ladies and gentleman. The Pyramid beckons, the Awards await our surprise and delight, and the day's light fades."

"Do you think Don's all right?" Penny asked.

"Oh, I imagine so," her husband replied as he and everyone else at the table stood. A moment later the patrons at all the other tables also stood. Max retrieved his flower box—he wasn't sure if he'd need to show an actual sample of his work, but he wasn't taking any chances.

"Well," Penny said, "he's awfully absent-minded. But on Awards Night?"

"Perhaps just another case of accute constipation," Brandon said.

"But it's been days!"

"Just like last time, if I recall. Shall we proceed?"

Max reached for his wallet, but Brandon waved a hand. "Nonsense, we have dined on my account. After all, an artist must watch his coin, eh? Hah hah! Ho ho! By God, I'm feeling much better!"

4. The dance of dances

Sool Koobie kneeled close to a wall of his cave, a bone tube in one hand, the fingertips of the other red with paint, his mouth full of spit and charcoal. The wall's red bricks were smooth with age, shiny with the greasy smears of Sool's shoulders in constant passage, and now crowded in painted images of the various spirits Sool had freed over the years— freed being Sool's unconscious euphemism for murdered in cold blood. Overhead, the cave's roof, consisting of woven detritus and misshapen pieces of corrugated aluminum, drummed and rustled beneath the night's light rain. The occasional rivulet dribbled down onto the smeared cobblestone floor, pooling close to the manhole cover, which led down into Sool's own private world of nether spirits and odd, bloodstained tubes of gauze that Sool threaded together to make his dancing cloak of death, which he now wore in homage to the god who was art, the gifts that were red ochre and charcoal paint, and the demonic angel who raced inside his head and gave painful birth to the images he now fashioned on the wall of his cave.

His was a world of magic, of gestures that were sacred, of dreams that were stories, and memories that were truth. In his propitiations before the hunt, and in the images he painted now the hunt was done, Sool had no sense of past or present, for each belonged to the central, tactile, physical truth that was the hunt itself.

Setting the tube to his lips, Sool leaned close to the wall and softly sprayed the wet charcoal, prescribing the curving sweep of Don

Palmister's back, then the heart line—the perspective a perfect rendition of what had met his eyes moments before he'd driven the spear home. With the red ochre paint in his other hand, he daubed on the flesh, the hint of muscle beneath the corduroy hide, the colour that was life and earth. In moments he was done. He spat out what was left of the charcoal, wiped the paint from his hand on his thigh and buttocks, adjusted the gauze-tube cloak, then cocked his head with a tense, febrile motion.

In the air, in the wet wind that drifted in from outside! A herd of vegetarians! A herd so large, so close! Sool Koobie's flesh quivered. A low whimper escaped his blackened lips. He spun into a flurry of gauze and beads and braids, the world in his perfect mind plunging into a dance of exaltation, communal propitiation, perfunctory mass extermination. The dance carried him into ecstacy, as he felt the spirits gathering, joining his flesh, surging through his veins and arteries.

And the sky blackened overhead, and thunder rumbled, and lightning flashed, and a neanderthal turned his glittering, narrow, red-rimmed eyes upon the world outside, and thought of death.

5. Discoveries

Annie waited below with her three bodyguards and the limo, but Andy "Kit" Breech gave little consideration to their likely impatience with this delay. He kneeled in the closet, the door open, the shoes flung out and lying on the living-room rug behind him, the secret trapdoor pried open, and the strange, mysterious electronic array spread out before him. *Headphones, with an impossibly long headband between the speakers . . . who the hell makes headphones for octopods!? A flat box, a round keyboard with strange symbols imprinted on each key, dials, switches, VU meters, frequency-finders. An aerial, wireless, made and sold by Radio Shack. A calculator, Texas Instruments, with tryg functions and expanded memory, a diagram with pencilled arc calculations, tensile strengths, velocity projections, angles, stress factors for some kind of mineral. Jottings, obscure notations, my God, what is all this?*

"Asap, give me a memo, please, help," Andy babbled, pulling at his lower lip. He found a second diagram, illustrating—with a precise hand— *no, tentacle—*a condom. *What? Stress calculations, elasticity factors, probability curves.* He clambered out of the closet, realizing he was gibbering wordlessly but not caring, and crawled up to the aquarium. Kit wouldn't meet his eye. The octopus lounged under its rock, glutted with a half-pound of calamari, and slowly twirled one tentacle tip with another; still another tentacle tapped slowly in time on the gravel bottom, and still another held up its huge . . . *head, or body, or whatever that blob's called. I used to know. I used to know everything about octopods. I used to ooze confidence when detailing my wonderful pet to each and every woman I brought up here— they'd see the incredible sensuality octopods exude, the strength of their sinuous limbs, the quiet awareness in their eyes, their startling explosiveness when they pounced—and they'd all damn near drag me into bed, wrapping themselves around me and grunting and gasping and begging—but now, but now I don't know anymore. I don't know anything. I feel weak, sucked clean, impotent. What can I do?*

Then suddenly he knew exactly what he was to do. "Kit," he hissed darkly. "When I get back, it's down the toilet with you. You brought it on yourself, Kit. You've left me no choice. You're pike meat, Kit. Sorry, old friend, but this is what it's come to, after all these years."

The intercom buzzed again, and Annie's tinny-squeezed voice called out, "Andeee! Please, lovemuffin! We'll be late! And Stubble needs to pee! Why didn't you go with the minister? We weren't expecting this detour, Andeee. Hurry down, please!"

The minister. Ride with him? With those pigeons trying to nail him every minute? You must be insane. Oh no, no way. He scrambled to his feet and stabbed the intercom button. "On my way, darling," he said.

At the door he paused one last time to glare at Kit. The octopus had edged to the corner of the aquarium, and was watching him, waiting for him to leave. *It's all connected. I know it is. I just thought my underwear was stretching, but that wasn't it. My penis is shrinking, my testicles are withdrawing, the hair's all falling out. I think you've been poisoning my condoms, Kit. Is it jealousy? Are you, uh, gay? This can't go on—I didn't even notice the last time I had a hard-on—I can't keep making excuses, my answer phone's full, the bitches are getting nastier with every message they leave. I just hide in here, staring at you. I can't think. I can't do anything. You've got to be . . . removed, Kit. I never thought you'd be the one to betray me. The fatal kiss, the taste of your salty beak on my lips. Et tu, Kitay?*

Heart-broken but with a new resolution, Andy left the apartment.

6. Escape!

Jojum was the biggest bruiser Joey "Rip" Sanger had ever seen. Of course, size was irrelevant, but it looked like the man could back it all up—he had fists that looked like stone mauls, and damn near the same colour too. And yet, there he stood, delicately, beautifully guiding the steam engine through the darkness, his touch a caress on the controls, his piggy eyes squinting into the darkness ahead.

Joey had been tied to a grab rail opposite the control station where Jojum sat. The knots were secure, the ropes unyielding. Gully and the other two scrubs had gone back to one of the other cars, leaving Jojum, just Jojum, but Joey knew it'd be enough. In any case, he was trussed up so tight he could barely breathe.

Joey tried talking. "Ain't no point in holdin' me, if ya think about it. Gully's got a problem, and it's me, and sooner or later he'll have to drop the black glove at my feet, and then the short straw will need picking. But I know Gully—I know people just like him. All heart and fairness to keep you sops in line, nodding your heads to whatever crap he delivers, but picking that straw won't be blind chance, Jojum. He'll have squirrelled the whole thing, and it's my guess he's already picked you out to do the job. You're big, and dumb—as far as he's concerned. He's the brain and you're the meat, and the meat does what the brain directs. You'll end up with a murder rap, Jojum, and Gully will be clean grease sliding off into the sunset. You're young, boy, but I ain't. I seen enough in my day to know what I'm looking at—this here cozy world Gully's devised, well, he's the emperor, ain't he? King Shit of Turd Mountain, right? You're here to stroke his ego, all of you, and t'make him feel virtuous. So he's cleaned the homeless off the streets—that's exactly what the powers that be want—to not see you, so they don't have to think about you, so they don't have to do anything about you. If Gully's rich, it's cause he's being paid outa the premier's pocket, mark my words."

Jojum slowly slid his flat gaze over at Joey. He blinked. "You say something, bud? My hearing ain't too good. Say, that's two nice shiners you got there, bud."

"Oh, bloody hell," Joey swore.

There was a shout and all of a sudden Wild Bill Chan was clambering up Jojum to batter at the man's head, and the Red Cap was clambering in through the entranceway, knife in hand and slicing at Joey's bonds.

"Hot damn!" Joey laughed.

Jojum and Chan were having a real set-to, grunting and grimacing and clobbering at each other, staggering back and forth, crashing into things, breaking things . . .

The ropes fell away and Joey leapt to his feet. "Hey!" he yelled at the two fighting men. "You two! Cut that out! Quit it, or you'll—"

Jojum slammed into the controls, snapping the handles at the far forward position. The train jolted, its wheels screaming, the dark scene outside quickly sliding past in a blur. Then Jojum, Chan clinging to him, caromed into the Red Cap, then Joey, and the fight got interesting for a while. Eventually Joey managed to pull himself away—he looked at the broken controls, then out the window. The Red Cap crawled to his side.

"Now we've gone and done it!" Joey swore. "We got ourselves a runaway train, and we're all dead men!"

Jojum and Chan stopped fighting briefly to look over at Joey and the Red Cap—the boy's face was white with fear, since the train was already going too fast to jump off—then the two men resumed their battle royale. Joey thought about joining in again, but Chan and Jojum seemed perfectly matched, and looked to be having fun besides.

Joey sighed. "Cheer up, Red Cap," he said, patting his pocket, "you're as close to earning your fiver as you've ever been."

7. Revelation!

Arthur Revell stumbled down the dark, wet street, alternately groaning and cursing. He'd swelled, burst through his clothing, and was now able to glare in through the dimly lit windows on the second floor of the buildings he staggered past. Just for fun he punched out a few, leaving a wake of ringing alarms. His horns had grown long and they itched, as if eager for goring, for rending flesh in a splash of fatal blood. "Gimme a Glenlivet!" he bellowed at the storm sky overhead, then kicked a parked car across to the other side of the street. He paused to stare at its crumpled remains, then grinned. "Cheap, smelly cigars," he rasped. "Days without bathing, picking my nose in public, farting in restaurants, aargh!"

What's happening to me? What am I becoming?

He heard sirens approaching from behind. Arthur spun around, spied the flashing lights. He picked up a garbage cannister—the kind that trucks hoisted up and tipped into their backsides—and flung it at the patrol car. There was a huge crash, then an explosion. "Aaargh!" Arthur crowed, shaking his fists. He threw his shoulder against an old brownstone building, felt its foundations crack, heard all the crap inside rattle, shatter and tinkle.

I am the ills of the nation! Awake with sour, deadly disposition. You all asked for it, every damn one of you, whoever you really are. Walls? I'll smash down your walls. Barricades? I'll crush them underfoot. Armoured personnel carriers? One slash of my serrated tail and you'll be flying in ruin. Welfare cuts? I'll take what I need. Taxman at the door? I'll rend him limb from limb. Budget cuts in every social service left to us? I'll devour the banks—crunch crunch crunch—I'll incinerate the legislative assemblies, the house of parliament, the cronies on the boards, the bloodless technocrats and vampire lawyers, the money-hoarders, the multinational forestry companies, oil companies, insurance companies, chain restaurants, mall designers, pharamceutical companies, cut-price food stores, trucking companies, corrupt unions, reformers, liberals, conservatives, separatists, unionists, lobbyists, bureaucrats, puritans, fanatic joggers, antismoking groups, antidrug groups, bad televi-

sion shows, the cynical, blood-hungry media. You've all made me ill. Terribly ill. I'm at the end of my rope, choking for want of compassion, humanity, common sense, and the end—god the end—to lies!

Arthur now towered over the core's turn-of-the-century buildings. He could see the dome of the legislature, he could see the peak of the Unified Cultural Workers Assembly Hall, and the skyscrapers housing the multinational companies and their tonnes and tonnes of useless paper and files and statistics and rules and prohibitions and secret codes—the reams of supposed authority, the chains of a dubious civilization, the bullshit breeding flies of misery and despair to a downtrodden, self-destructing species.

"My God," he breathed. "I know what I am. I know what I've become! It's all clear to me now, at last. I'm awake, at last awake, and the world will shake! The towers will topple! I am the monster you created, the one whose awakening you dreaded, sought to impede, tried to ignore—but it's too late! Aaargh! And aargh again! What will you do now that I'm awake, eh? Eh? EH? EEEHHHH! You see, I know what I am now! Finally! I'm an artist! AAARRGHHH!!!"

His sights set on the legislature buildings and the corporate castles, Arthur Revell began his rampage of destruction.

8. Liberation at last at last

In the way of octopods, Kit squeezed through the last keyhole and flopped out down onto the floor. He raised himself up on his eight legs and looked around. Silence, an apartment asleep in the absence of its owner. Outside the wind howled, thunder boomed, lightning flashed.

Kit slimed his way into the bedroom, moving from one cover to the next, darting and sploshing and oozing, and arrived at the dresser drawer. He opened it and extracted the large box of condoms. The box tucked under one arm, Kit returned to the living room.

The radio equipment had proved a perfect decoy. Andrew was confused. It was important that Andrew be confused, allowing Kit to complete his preparations. Squatting in the sunken living room, Kit opened the box and began ripping open the plastic envelopes of condoms, one after another, until he had on the rug in front of him six hundred and thirty-two slippery, rubbery, multicoloured tubes. Then he began tying one to the next, fashioning a rope of remarkable elasticity.

This completed, Kit carried the rope to the balcony door, which he unlocked and slid to one side. He slipped out onto the balcony, quickly knotted one end of the rope to the wrought-iron railing, and then the other end as well. He paused, turned to stare across the intervening distance to the balcony on the building opposite, and to the lovely pooch that sat there, watching him. Kit waved. The pooch's ears pricked up, its tail thumped once.

Kit returned to his task. He positioned himself in the centre of the condom rope, then, using all his strength, and reaching for each carefully arranged piece of furniture, Kit pulled himself across the floor towards the closet door. The rope stretched tight around his soft body, but he contracted his muscles against it and kept on crawling, inching ever closer to the closet.

He finally reached it, wrapping the tip of each tentacle around the doorknob. The rope, now a slingshot, hummed taut across the length of the apartment. Kit slowly worked himself around until he was facing the open balcony door. He ran through the calculations once again in his mind, set his beak in a determined tight line, then let go.

The doorway flashed by in a blur, then he was out, flying through the air, the apartment and the balcony opposite him growing big alarmingly fast. He splayed out his eight tentacles, felt the elastic webbing between each limb fill with air, braking his murderous speed. He saw the pooch cock it head, its eyes widening as Kit raced straight for him. The dog ducked at the last moment and Kit splatted into the glass door behind it, then slid down to a crumpled heap on the balcony floor.

The pooch looked down at Kit. At the first sign of movement, her tail thumped once.

Kit shook himself, then podded himself upright. The dog licked him on the forehead and Kit sent two tentacles around the sweet quadruped in a brief, but emotional hug, then he clambered swiftly onto the dog's back. He settled himself in, reached up and slid aside the glass door.

"Is that you, Moopsy?" a quavering voice asked from inside.

Kit kicked Moopsy's flanks and they entered. An old woman sat on the sofa, blinking bemusedly at the two of them. "Have you found a date, then?" she asked. "Oh, I'm so proud of you, Moopsy. Be sure to be home before dawn, dear, you know how I'll worry."

Kit guided Moopsy to the door, freeing one tentacle to wave at the old woman before they left. Time had come, at last, to paint the town red.

9. *And they shall be rewarded*

Max stood with Brandon, Lucy and Penny at the foot of the steps to the Unified Cultural Workers Assembly Hall. "That's a lot of steps," he said, eyeing the climb.

"Six hundred and sixty-six, my soon-to-be-marginally-famous friend. Keeps out the riffraff, you see. The appreciation of art demands hard work, as you well know. Anything casually, easily received is crass commercialism, and let's not be naive, such practitioners exist in this city, though of course we'll never acknowledge them. I can think of one off the top of my head, which is something in itself—"

Eyeing Brandon's expanding head, Max had to agree.

"—I believe her name is Elana Oxbow, her only positive feature being she is of a visible minority. Native, I believe. Despite that, her primary interest seems to be increasing her audience in size and appreciation. Can you imagine anything so . . . vulgar, but more than that, Maximillian, she's also plum dangerous, a threat to our subtle way of life."

"I hate her," Lucy squeaked from beside Brandon's knee. "She should die, I think. That's what I think, and what I think is more important than you think, unless you think the way I think, making us think alike and are you thinking what I'm thinking, that's what I want to know."

"Indeed," Brandon rumbled. "We should be on our way."

"Ooh," Penny cried. "Here comes Annie and Andy and Monk and Stubble and Nick. And a helicopter—that must be the minister, oh, what timing!"

Annie's limo rolled up and those inside climbed out. The thunder and lightning continued overhead, along with the occasional gust of wind, but it seemed the rain had passed, and the late spring air was turning sultry. Annie waved and, followed by her three bodyguards, approached. Andy hesitated by the limo, torn by some kind of indecision. Another limo approached, and the helicopter had landed, crushing a bag lady but otherwise uneventfully, and now waited, its props whirring.

Curious, Max watched. The limo stopped perilously close to the helicopter. The black vehicle looked battered, dented, with blots of feather stuck to it here and there. The door opened and the minister bolted, racing across the intervening space for the helicopter. The props made a strange *budding* noise and the night air was filled with grey feathers, and then the minister was inside, and Andy "Kit" Breech was heading up to it at a more leisurely pace. He leaned into the cockpit and exchanged a few words with the minister, then turned and made his way towards the group.

Max swung his attention back to those who'd gathered around Brandon. Annie was speaking. " . . . and I really figured there'd be some kind of takeover bid at CAPSs, but Monk here intercepted two frustrated artists in the foyer. He castrated the man—" her nose wrinkled momentarily— "rather messily, in my opinion, and intellectually raped the other, who was female, it turned out."

Max couldn't help himself. "Intellectually raped, Annie?"

She nodded. "At gun point, he forced her to knit a feminist quilt, right then and there, until she finally broke down and started foaming at the mouth. It was quite exciting, actually. Anyway, that's why we were late, that and picking up Andy—who's not well at all tonight, are you, Andy?"

Max looked over at the man, of whom he'd heard only hints of rumours, suggesting that here stood the real power behind everything. An assistant deputy to the minister, or some such thing, a bureaucrat, a technocrat, a lifer in the game. The man looked like hell, and threw Annie an ill-disguised scowl when her words drew everyone's attention to him.

"I'm fine," he growled. "The minister will join us inside."

"Excellent," Brandon said.

They all turned to watch the helicopter rise from the street and skim up the steps to the Pyramid's landing platform on the roof.

"Shall we ascend, then?" Brandon asked the group, with a broad smile. "Come on, climb aboard."

Max stared as Lucy, her bulky, heavy handbag in tow, climbed onto Brandon's left thigh, wrapping her arms and legs around the tree-trunk-like bole of muscle and bone. Then Penny moved up and settled into Brandon's arms. Annie positioned herself piggyback behind his broad shoulders. Brandon grinned over at the remaining men. "You'll all have to walk, I'm afraid, because I'm all man and certain things are just not done. I'm sure you can manage, hah hah! Ho ho! Tally ho!"

Brandon took the first steps two at a time, then three, then five, then ten, then twenty, leaping upward in powerful bounds, the hair on his massive head waving in the wind of his swift, effortless passage.

Max glanced over at Andy, who was still scowling. "I hear it's easier if you zigzag," he said helpfully.

Andy curled his lip. "Don't talk to me about zigzagging, you pup."

In a flurry of motion Monk, Stubble and Nick had their M-16's out and laid down a spraying fire into a crowd of boy scouts who'd edged too close in their annual litter-collecting drive. Innocent voices screamed.

"Cut that out!" Andy bellowed.

The guns stuttered into silence, leaving a moaning pile of youthful bodies buried in black plastic and litter.

"I'm minded," Andy hissed, "to let the media hang you all on this one!"

The three helmeted men hung their heads.

"But," Andy continued in a rasping tone, "I'm in a generous mood tonight. Now get out the climbing gear—Annie's feeling lost and fearful for her life without you at her back. Hop to it. As for you, Maxipad, get climbing —I'll be stuck to your tail like used toilet paper, count on it— because I'll tell you right now, I don't trust you."

"Oh," Max said. "But I've brought one of my sculptures." He lifted the flower box.

"You think I give a shit, boy? Now climb."

They arrived at the glass and steel entranceway fifteen minutes later, Max drenched in sweat and seriously winded. Other guests had gathered around an oxygen tent set up just inside the doors, while paramedics worked desperately and, it seemed, unsuccessfully on another quest to a side of the landing. As Max crouched at the last step, kneading out a stitch in his side, and Andy stood unruffled and barely pink cheeked beside him, the three bodyguards arrived like a SAS team, on ropes, with grappling hooks, and in urban assault formation. They quickly took stock of the situation, checked their private frequency helmet transmitters, then headed inside to find Annie.

"Don't get near me inside," Andy told Max. "Don't even look in my direction. Got it?"

"Uh, yeah, right."

"Fine. Now get out of my sight."

Nodding, Max collected his flower box and staggered inside.

A few hundred of the city's select crowded the high-ceilinged hallway, recovering with glasses of white wine and nibblets provided by Culture Quo, which were brought to them individually by starving artists working part-time as waiters and waitresses. Off to the right was the entrance to the theatre, where the awards would be handed out, but that was still an hour away. Max scanned the crowd until he saw Brandon's massive head—a brown hump like the shoulders of a bison rising above all the other guests—and the knot of familiars around him. Max headed over.

"Don't fret, Lucy dear, dear Lucy," Brandon was saying, "I've ensured that the gaggle of critics are all seated in a single row, just as you requested. Right up at the front, as per your wishes, and thereby subject to your righteously baleful gaze throughout the proceedings." It seemed Lucy would be sitting up at the front, on the stage platform, along with other important personages, including the minister, Andy, Penny and Annie. Max had been provided a seat along an aisle towards the back, thus ensuring a long, momentous approach down to collect his award. "Ahh, Maxmillian my friend, I'm glad to see you survived the ordeal of the steps without much discomfort, such is youth, eh? Hah hah! Ho ho! Well, I must ready myself for the task at hand, so I will leave you for now, in the capable and expressive hands of my darling wife. Cheerio! The next time you see me will be as Emcee, standing in the spotlight, my smile warm and my confidence emanating from every pore of my body, hah hah! Ho ho!"

He strode off, the crowd parting before him.

Max saw Annie receive a cellular phone. She listened, frowned, then gestured her three bodyguards closer. She gave them whispered, heated instructions, her face pale, and the men saluted, checked their gear, then headed off. Max followed them with his gaze, as they found a door to a service elevator, Monk keying in a code. All three scrambled inside when the doors opened, and Max watched as the lights indicated their descent, down, down into the bowels of the structure.

Penny accidentally kneed Lucy into the lowest shelf of a passing service cart and ignored her dwindling yelps as she edged close to Max and murmured, "Ready to perform for me tonight, darling?"

"Huh? Tonight? When, after you mean?"

"I was thinking right up there on stage. Imagine the glory as, in front of a thousand politicians, administrators, professors, and obscure but powerful artists, critics and media pundits, you were to install your art under my mnemonic mound—I'm almost certain that I was once Margaret Thatcher, you know—"

"But she isn't dead yet, Penny."

"She isn't? Oh. Well, Joan of Arc, then."

"Oh, well, she is dead, that's true. But, Penny—in public? I don't know if, uh, I can perform under that kind of—"

"Oh don't be silly," Penny said. "I'm just kidding, besides. We'll polish the tip of the Pyramid after it's over, out under the stormy sky—"

"Sounds uncomfortable—"

She smiled. "For you, maybe. Oops, what's Annie all heated up about?"

Max turned to see the chief administrator sharply gesticulating for them to join her. She had a set of earphones on, and looked to be in great excitement. "We'd better see," Max said.

They headed over.

"Someone's down below," Annie hissed. "An intruder. I sent the boys down to take care of him—oh, I knew there'd be a try, a takeover bid, something unsightly and crass. Come with me, we'll head to the security room and we can hear all the gory details—I've given the boys carte blanche!''

The security room housed a bank of television monitors, and a com station. A technician sat at the station and nodded to Annie when they entered. He flicked a switch and removed his headphones as, through a vague buzz of speaker static, one of the bodyguard's voices whispered, "Nick? Where the hell are ya, buddy? Shit!"

A second voice broke in. "It's Stubble, what's your position, Monk?"

"Coordinates 16G, level four. I sent Nick ahead—the tunnel's had its lights busted out. Now I can't reach him. You listening up there, Com? Check your cameras down corridor 32, switch to IR."

The technician flicked more switches. "Roger that, Monk. Going visual on my mark—you scoped?"

"No, dammit, there's a bug in the system— you're my eyes, friend."

"Don't worry," the technician said, "I'll pull you through. Okay . . . mark!" He pushed a button and a monitor to his left flickered. A heat blob was crouched over another one, the one on the floor swiftly cooling. The blob straightened, looked directly at the camera, then snapped out a hand. A black chunk of something flew up at the lense, then there was static.

Annie gasped. The technician now leaned forward in his chair. "Monk, you reading me? Over?"

"Yeah, what's up?"

"Your boy's down. Intruder is heading your way. Head's up—"

"It's Stubble! Pull back, Monk, until I can support ya! Pull back!"

Monk said, "I see something—no, just a shadow—no, what, wait— shit!" There was a burst of machine gun fire, then a scream, then the hiss of static.

Stubble spoke, "Monk? Hey bruiser, you hearing me? Nailed the bastard, eh? Monk? Come in, Monk, over. Monk?"

The technician activated a second screen, sweat trickling down his brow. The image that came up was a floorplan of level four. A signatured heat blob was visible near the stairs, slowly edging towards Monk's last known position. Stubble, Max realized. Then he and the others saw another smudge of heat, moving swiftly on an intercept course. "Stubble!" the technician screamed. "He's coming straight for you!"

"Where? Shit! Where, dammit—I don't see a damn thing!"

Max stared as the two heat blobs merged.

Stubble was shrieking in terror. "I don't see! Where, fuck, where—aaghhh!" Again a burst of machine gun fire, then nothing but static.

In the security room, Max and Penny and Annie and the technician watched in horrified silence as the blob made its way to the stairs, entered, and disappeared from the screen.

"Find him again!" Annie screamed.

But the technician shook his head. "Budget restraints," he said. "We had the overall IR network set up for levels six to four, but then we ran out of money. He's taking out the cameras, too. We've lost him."

"My God," Penny whispered. "And he's on his way, and there's not a thing we can do to stop him!"

From outside a bell gonged.

Annie cast Max a frightened glance, then straightened. "The show must go on. There's only one of him. I'll be right at the front. The minister's guards are there, behind the curtain—you, too, Penny—we'll be safe." She looked at Max with pity in her eyes. "Sorry, Max."

He shook his head, already resigned. "At least I've been warned," he said, "and that's more than anyone else can say out there."

"Good point," Annie said. "Keep your mouth shut, and you should be all right, just get ready to, uh, run, I guess."

"Right."

They quickly left the security room, leaving the technician furiously trying to track the intruder—with no chance of success.

Max found his seat, then sat and watched as Penny and Annie appeared on the stage and seated themselves behind the long table where they joined the minister, Andy and the top of Lucy's head—which is all that was visible even from Max's vantage point. The assembly hall was packed, voices filling the air in a droning murmur.

A burst of applause greeted Brandon Safeword's approach to the podium. He inclined his prodigious head and smiled out at the guests. "A wonderful evening, ladies and gentlemen," he intoned, "in which to celebrate the achievements of this city's talented, brilliant artists, all of whom saw their start as recipients of funding from Culture Assessment Promotional Support services—which we affectionately know as CAPSs. Not that such funding is a prerequisite to the receipt of tonight's awards—most certainly not, hah hah, ho ho!—rather," he leaned forward on the podium, "it is indicative of CAPSs remarkable percipience at finding and supporting artists of exceptional ability, no matter which university they might have attended!

"Now," he continued, smiling broadly, "first a word or two about the panel of peers, who for the past eight months have struggled with the difficult task of choosing tonight's award winners. Each judge in his or her own right is an artist of renown and admiration. Since you all know them, I'll simply recount the List of Lists using only their first names. The position of chair, this year, hath been held with honour by dear Margie, who was a student who knew Donny and in union begat six grants and four major awards; whereupon Margie was gifted with a suitable post at the university, and came in time to know Chuck, Samuel and Peter, and in the knowing thereof begat nineteen various awards and grants. In Chuck, knowing in time Elizabeth and Sally—though in each knowing an interval of time doth exist between the two, allowing for lawful propriety in the knowing thereof, was begat in twin succession twenty-two awards and grants; and in the gathering thereof, Chuck came to know Donny who begat funding for Samuel, who knew Sally and begat funding for Elizabeth, who knew Margie once more and begat funding for Peter, who then knew Donny and begat funding for Margie, who came in knowing to Lucy, and so knowingly doth Lucy begat Peter who, in begatting with knowing Elizabeth, begat Chuck, who remained at this time in the knowing with Samuel, Margie and Donny, thus allowing in proper prescription the gathering of those in knowing, mainly these being the panel of peers who in all knowing begat the awards on this here night on behalf of nameless donors, a multitude of taxpayers, a slice of lottery funding, minus administrative fees and the knowing task of begatting, which in itself is known to be a costly thing; thus minus said trimmings these awards nevertheless being nearly a month's salary for said peers in their knowing universities and tenure and so worthy of sustaining an artist or two for a year maybe longer, we all begat in knowing the knowingly known, though some may not be known as yet by this night's end all shall be known at least in knowing circles of import and sacred truths, of which there are many and by swearing loyalty shall remain unwritten and so unopposable in the eyes of the public. Amen."

"Amen!" the crowd murmured.

"And now," Brandon continued, "for your unrestrained enjoyment, professor Lucy Mort shall read an excerpt from her most recent work, *Mommy Mommy Mommy.* Ladies and gentlemen, Professor Lucy Mort . . ."

The crowd roared. The crowd was on its feet—not in ovation, but in an effort to discern the tiny creature that scurried up to disappear behind the podium. Brandon quickly adjusted the goose-neck microphone until it too was out of sight. The crowd slowly sat back down, and silence fell.

A moment later a tiny voice cleared its throat, and the words followed,

I shun you and him and her and them
for not giving me the golden pen
I shun rivals for the almighty dosh
and the critics who despise my success
I shun for not giving me attention
I shun too, because it's fun!

There followed a silent moment, then one of the critics at the front shouted out, "What the hell has that got to do with mommies, Lucy dear?"

The crowd gasped.

Lucy jumped out from behind the podium, her head no bigger than an apple. She shrieked, "I'm not finished! That's why! Wait!" She jumped back to the microphone, and the sound of her desperate breathing echoed through the hall, then,

I shun too, because it's fun!

. . .

Isn't it, Mum?

Everyone cheered wildly, applauded frantically. Max stood with them, bashing his hands together and watching, along with everyone else, as Lucy climbed the tablecloth and stood up on the table in front of her chair. She reached down and hauled up her purse, which she unzipped, pulled out a tommy gun, and spun to the row of critics seated in front of her, and let them have it. The critics exploded in a messy expostulation of flesh, bone, blood, guts and a few bits of brain, along with upholstery and clothing bits and pieces of shoes and notepads and rotten tomatoes previously stored in paper bags. Smoking cartridges spun wildly from the tommy gun as Lucy—visibly struggling under its weight and getting smaller by the second—continued pumping rounds into the amalgamated, sliced, diced and ground-up critics, some of whom kept raising their hands to ask piercing questions revealing their sly, cynical erudition—but the gesture was wasted, and didn't in fact last much longer, as even the hands were pummelled into little bits. Then the gun was empty, and fell clattering onto the table in front of miniscule Lucy Mort.

At this moment the minister's six bodyguards were flung bodily through the curtain to flop and sprawl and roll and thump in blood-spewing messes onto the long table, knocking over every single pitcher of lemon water. And behind them appeared Sool Koobie, his sleek lithe body painted in frightening patterns, a hafted hand axe in one hand, his spear in the other, and wearing as his only item of clothing a long, billowy cloak of used tampons.

Annie, Penny, Andy, the minister and Brandon shrieked in unison, then scattered as, with a weird, terrifying, ululating yell, Sool Koobie rushed the assembly.

Max made no effort to join the stampede for the doors. Instead he clambered over the heads and shoulders of the knotted mob and reached the thick heavy curtain against the wall, which he climbed with the zeal of an ape, still clutching his flower box. Fifteen feet above the surging, screaming, murderously panicked crowd, he hung on for his life. He tried to shift the box under an arm but the lid opened and the submarine fell out, to land on the churning sea of coiffed heads below, where it slowly rocked and wobbled its way out through the exit. "Shit!" Max hissed. "Doesn't matter now though, does it? Holy cow, look at that guy!"

Sool Koobie was slaying with wild abandon, cleaving vegetarians in twain right and left, driving the herd ever forward to the two narrow choke points of the hall's exits. Max scanned the overturned table on the stage but saw no one. Meanwhile, the savage leapt everywhere, laying out red ruin wherever he landed and crooning eerily with every killing blow he delivered.

And yet the whole scene since Lucy's lead-filled refutation of the critics had lasted but a few seconds. All of a sudden Max found himself alone— the crowd had been driven out of the hall—and the screams continued as Sool pursued them. Max looked down, scanned the inert bodies below, seeing a few moaning and writhing in their death wounds, then falling still. Bodies, everywhere, bodies. He turned in his perch as he heard voices up at the front. There stood Brandon and Lucy, looking unscathed.

"There there Lucy dear," Brandon was saying.

"I'm out of bullets!" Lucy wailed. "And I can't even hold up the gun anymore! Oh, Brandon, what am I going to do! There's commercial artists out there, all more successful than me! I have to kill them! I have to, Brandon!"

"Of course, dear, of course. But you're in luck—I have a penknife!"

"Give it to me!"

He handed it down to her.

"I'm off!" She leapt down from the stage and raced up the body-littered aisle.

"But where, dear?" Brandon called out. "Where?"

"Chesterton's!" she squeaked. "Thursday's Lounge! That's where I'll find them! They're dead! All of them, dead!"

Max watched her pass beneath him, then slowly climbed down. That savage would likely be back, collecting trophies, finishing the last ones off. He had to get out of the Pyramid. But something made him pause at the exit and turn back to where Brandon still stood.

"Hey!" Max called, knowing the jig was up, the entire jig, and not giving a damn anymore. "Hey, Brandon!"

The majormacrocephalic man looked up. "Maximillian! Well done!"

"I know all about your brother, Brandon!" Max yelled gleefully.

"He's a big star back east! Bigger than you'll ever be in this squat little piss hole! Hah hah ho ho!"

Brandon froze, the veins bulged, the head swelled and swelled, and then, as he screamed his white rage, the head exploded, spraying styrofoam chips everywhere. The body staggered, the hands groped, found the curtain, swept it aside, then the body ran away, disappearing from sight.

Max grinned, feeling better than he'd felt in years.

10. *From on high*

Wild Bill Chan and Jojum had tied themselves up into an immovable knot that lay against the engine's back hatch, forcing John Gully to grunt with great effort as he pushed his way inside. He swiftly scanned the scene, his gaze coming to rest first on the broken controls, then on Joey.

Joey "Rip" Sanger shrugged. "An accident. Told you ya shoulda left me alone, or doused me right at the start. And now we're barrelling along, outa control who knows where—"

"I do," Gully said. "We're heading into the city. We'll never make the turn before the station. There's gonna be one hell of a mess."

Joey shrugged again. "It was bound to happen, Gully. Screwing with the laws of nature, you've been, and now the piper's called your due."

"The laws of nature?" Gully sat down on the floor, his back resting against the control sleeve. "What on earth are you talking about, Mr Sanger?"

"There'll always be poor," Joey growled. "Y'can hide 'em, y'can squirrel 'em away and get slipped the cool green by the powers that be, y'can pretend yer doin good with this here housin' scheme a yours, but it's all pissing in the wind, Gully. Y'got the ones that have, and the ones that ain't, but want. Every now and then they have a set-to, at each other's throats—the ones that have defendin' territory, the ones that ain't trying t'carve out a piece for themselves. And maybe it turns right over, the faces switchin' right around, but you know what? Nothing changes. I figured you for a smarter buck than that, Gully, but you're just fooling 'em all, yourself included."

Gully sighed. "You missed the entire point, Mister Sanger. Missed it by a mile. I'm not interested in getting my people to change places with those on high. My plans, which you have succinctly ruined this night, were far more profound, far more potentially devastating. I lead the Fruitful Church of Disobedience, Mister Sanger—"

"Oh, hell, anarchists!"

Gully shrugged. "People—all of us—got messed up in the fifties, and we've been thinking and trying to get back to those days ever since. But it was a sham back then: the prosperity was singular, a blip in history's miserable line. It was false—the economy, even the society with all its icons shoved on us by television. Nuclear families? Mum, Dad, the kids and the dog? Oh, really. Look at the history of our species. Kids were meant to be raised communally. Aunts, uncles, grandparents, cousins. No single woman—or man—was ever considered to be wholly responsible. Tack on a nine-to-five job, then two of them, and you've got one royal fuck-up that burned itself out within a single generation. Hence the sixties, and now the nineties, with that artificial construct all falling apart under immense, unreasonable pressures and unrealistic expectations. Single mums, single dads, screwed-up kids—it's all falling to pieces. And everyone walks around blaming each other, blaming the neighbours, the crackpots, the criminals, the strangers down the block. Tougher on crime, tougher on panhandlers, tougher and still tougher, keep breeding the paranoia, keep making isolated entities of us all, divide and conquer, divide and divide and divide, until we all feel powerless, dependent, until dignity disappears from the common tongue. Today's leaders—politicians and businessmen—have pulled off what kings and emperors and high priests only dreamed of in the back when. At least in the old days people knew when they were just meat, gristle, muscle and bone and nothing else. Now, everyone still believes they count for something, even when they know that that something is one big lie. And so we keep trudging on, trying to make sense of things, trying to achieve the unachievable, sticking to the rules—most of us—and thinking that it all serves something important, but what it serves is the cronies on top and no one else."

"Yeah yeah yeah," Joey said. "Big deal. So you want to tear it all down, start from scratch, but the guy who's missing the point is you. You got too much faith in human nature, Gully. You think we ain't naturally depraved, naturally vicious, naturally assholes—and that's your mistake, and it's a doozy."

"Of course we're all those things!" Gully snapped. "Doesn't mean we can't strive for something better!"

"In your dreams, Gully, and nowhere else."

"Ohmigod," the Red Cap whispered, his eyes widening on what he could see out the side window. "We're coming to the bend, and that's not all— there's a monster out there, twenty storeys tall at least, tearing up buildings, batting down helicopters and fighter jets!"

Gully leaned out the window, then stepped back, looking thoughtful.

Joey followed suit. "Yup," he said, "that's one big bastard. Wonder who he is?"

"Arthur Revell," Gully said. "I know him only marginally, it's true, but I don't think I'm mistaken. He's . . . changed."

"Let me guess, the horns are new."

Gully glanced over at Joey, his expression becoming animated. "There's your destroyer, Joey! He's discovered his inner self, who he is deep down inside, and now we're all going to pay!"

"Why, what is he?"

"An artist!"

"My God," Joey breathed, experiencing terror for the first time since facing Sool Koobie. "He's got to be stopped!"

"It's too late!" the Red Cap screamed, just as the racing train finally arrived at the bend. The 57 Wells engine seemed to leap from the rails, dragging the mass of cars with it, down the gentle slope giving the bend its rise, ploughing up two huge waves of gravel, clinkers, dust and sand—then, the engine reaching a street, the cow-catcher carved a swath through the concrete, then bucked upward—and the train of homeless victims was plummeting down the city's main street, flinging hapless cars to either side, barrelling with unstoppable momentum straight for the legislative buildings a mere seven blocks distant.

Arthur Revell was suffering from an orgylike explosion of lifelong chemical deprivation—no alcohol slurring his veins and arteries, no nicotine hammering his heart, no tar clogging up his lungs, no cocaine from postperformance parties, no acid from wild-eyed friends, no hash, no grass, no hemp, no peyote, no ecstacy, no speed, no mushrooms—he was in the hell of purified creativity, undulled by the oral/anal compulsive obsessions that strung out the spirit and forced on the body and mind a more reasonable pace—no longer the tortoise, but the hare; not a cicada but a moth speeding to the flame. Arthur saw before him his brief, apocalyptic glory, and answered it with a roar of soul-searing frustration.

His burning eyes fixed on the legislative dome, and beyond that, the Pyramid, Arthur took one gigantic step forward, his talons curling with desire. He opened his mouth and a swarm of ladybugs poured forth in an eager, bloodythirsty cloud. He paused, confused, then—on a breath of cool wind, came a scent that froze him in his tracks. "Peaches!" he hissed. "I smell peaches! Faye! Faye!" Arthur whirled about, found the faint scent once again, then surged forward on its delicate, wonderful trail.

Maxwell Nacht stepped into the hall beyond the theater, and saw the remains of bloody chaos. The long tables on which sat the finest culinary profferings of Culture Quo, had been shattered, strawlike foodstuffs scattered everywhere. More bodies lay about, motionless, horribly motionless. The waiters and waitresses all crouched against the far wall, their eyes dulled, their mouths hanging open.

One of them spoke, "He—he didn't touch us. He came over and . . . sniffed us, then he left—he drove them on, on, ever onward!"

Max didn't spare them another glance. He went through the shattered entranceway and arrived at the landing. The wind gusted calmly across his sweat-beaded face. He looked below, down the six hundred sixty-six steps, and saw exactly what he expected to see. He also saw Penny off to one side, halfway down the steps—she looked up to him.

"My God!" she screamed. "The city's entire art establishment is dead!"

The savage had driven them, like buffalo, Max realized, off the steps— and Max could see the horrible little man, down there among the piled bodies, cutting out tongues, collecting ears and other delectible trophies. And now Penny saw him as well.

"Ohmigod!" Max heard her say. "She—she—she *remembers!* You! You down there! Oh, my noble one! You!"

The savage glanced up at all the screaming and watched bemused as the scantily-clad woman rushed towards him, down the steps, over the bodies, running straight for him, arms stretched out.

Sool Koobie bleated as Penny leapt on him, her legs spread wide.

Max stared as she writhed over the hapless creature.

"She remembers! Oh God she remembers! I'm—I'm—I'm . . . Croona! Queen of the Cavemen! I've come home! Home! Oh, take me take me take me take me!"

And Sool did, grabbing her thighs and boldly throwing her on her back, there atop the hundreds of dead politicians, professors, obscure but powerful artists, business leaders, he rogered Penny Foot-Safeword in the fashion of hunky, smelly, grunting primitive men the world over.

Max sighed, actually happy for them both, and wishing them well in whatever squalid hole the savage would no doubt drag Penny into. As for himself, well, enough of the loner jaunt, the gamble of youth—past at last for Maxwell Nacht of the Nacht Lingerie Empire. Time to go home to the millions, the swimming pools, the high society, the tennis lessons and the maids in the bushes. He'd had his fun pretending to be the artist, he was tired of going hungry, tired of the cockroaches on the kitchen counter, tired of mouldy bread and Kraft Dinner, and the endlessly arguing drunks on welfare next door. "I'm going home," he whispered. "Home, my God."

At precisely this moment the 57 Wells tore through the legislature, destroying everything, absolutely everything, including the late-night session where politicians of various stripes had been arguing with no one in particular against any reduction in personal pay, benefits, and the double-dipping loopholes in their fat pension plans. The huge steam engine retired them all, permanently, but the train didn't stop and indeed was only marginally slowed in its passage through the historical edifice.

Max could only watch as the mechanical demon plunged across the street and crashed into the six hundred sixty-six steps of the Pyramid, flinging bodies and concrete and dead boy scouts and, as the cars behind the engine piled up and burst apart, hundreds of homeless people flew in all directions, thus providing a demographic slice of modern Western society.

Even before the dust cleared, someone flashed by close to Max and scurried down the steps—a figure that seemed able to disappear as it turned sideways, blinking into and out of existence as it descended towards the rubble below.

The minister. Paul Silverthump. Nice trick, that sideways disappearing act. Beauty. The man's a born politician. Look, not even a hair out of place. Gotta admire the bastard. Hell, he's the only one left, too. Which means he'll be taking the reins of power shortly, before the dust down there's even settled. And who says God isn't just?

Eight hundred and twenty-three feet overhead in the smoke-filled darkness, a wheeling pigeon outfitted with infrared goggles spotted its target. The bird banked, folded back its wings, and dived.

Few regarded pigeons with much respect, it knew, a lack of which was about to be remedied in an act of singular, heroic self-sacrifice. The pigeon picked up even more speed, becoming nothing more than a blur of unstoppable intent, and it knew, in its last moments, that God was on its side, and failure was out of the question.

Max saw Paul Silverthump stop suddenly, entirely visible, and totter slightly on the steps. Something was sticking out of his head, fluttering darkly. Half a pigeon, in fact. The other half was embedded in the man's head, which even for a politician was likely fatal. And, true enough, Max watched the man topple limply onto the steps then slowly slide down to join the disaster scene below.

Sorry for ever doubting you, God. Never again, I promise. My God, I'm going to join a monastery! That'll put the old man in a tizzy! One hell of a tizzy! Hee hee!

Arthur Revell arrived at the hospital and saw her. The night shift, taking a smoke break outside the doors, dear Faye of the blushing bosom. His shadow swept over her and she looked up.

Arthur expected her to scream. It would have been an entirely natural response. Instead, she took one last, deep drag on her cigarette, flicked the butt to one side, and delicately held out her hand.

"I'm an artist!" Arthur boomed down at her.

"I know!" she said.

"I need—I need—I need—"

"I know! I know what you need, darling Arthur!" She pulled a metal flask from her hip, her pack of smokes from her pocket, and waved them both in the air over her head. "I'm a nurse, remember?"

Arthur straightened for one last roar, a roar of intent, as dark a promise as it had ever been, but this time it was also a roar of sheer joy. "I love life!" he bellowed. "Aaargh!"

On a poorly lit, emptied street, Kit dismounted, hobbled Moopsy, then approached, in great curiosity, the tiny woman riding the motorized submarine steadily down the street's centre. She held her penknife under one arm like a lance and was muttering something about commericial artists and wildlife painters lucky enough to be born Native.

Kit felt a surge of inevitability deep inside his generally amorphous body, as if a thousand instincts had been triggered at the sight that met his eyes. He slimed forward on an intercept course.

The woman screamed as the submarine's splayed nose rammed into Kit, who tried a scream of his own and was pleased at its shrill, bestial madness. His tentacles lashed out, gripping the submarine and holding it fast. Lucy Mort stood up and hefted the penknife, her legs spread out to keep balance on the pitching deck. "Die, bastard from the deep!" she yelled.

Idly, Kit reached up, flipped the puny penknife from her hands, encircled the woman and boldly lifted her into the air. Her arms thrashed, her hair tossed, her legs kicked, all with equal ineffectivity, and her last shriek was a tinny, hopeless cry, *"Help me! Help meeee!!"* Kit studied her a moment longer, then ate her in a blinding flash.

He finished the scene by shrilling some more and bashing the submarine into pieces, then he returned to Moopsy, who'd watched the whole thing with tail wagging. Kit mounted up, and they rode westward to their date with destiny.

Max sat on a piece of rubble and observed the proceedings. The media had arrived, adding to the chaos of the scene at the foot of the Pyramid's steps. What was worse, they'd found the homeless—most of whom had survived the crash, which had proved unlucky for them, as the media crews, upon discovering real homeless people, had descended on them with a flurry of heart-bleeding angst.

The predictable end result was being played out below. A woman stood above the still form of Jojum, dead from a microphone shoved down his throat. A cameraman stood opposite her, its mounted spot bathing the reporter and the body in heavenly light. "This is Sandy Grit, MFFB News, coming to you from the central scene of devastation, where an even greater tragedy has occurred. You see this man below me, a poor homeless man, victimized by— I have no choice but to acknowledge it— by a mindless, news-hungry media that views all humanity with a cold, cynical eye. I am ashamed to call myself part of this profession. My God, what have we become? All this just for ratings? For revenue? To shock and entice you with the depravity of modern civilization? Is that all we're here for? Well, let me tell you all right here and right now, MFFB isn't like the rest. We're not . . . animals, and we're not going to take it anymore! You'll see for yourself, my friends, soon enough, and that's a promise from Sandy Grit, coming to you live from the foot of the Pyramid."

The light blinked out.

"Move it!" the next reporter snarled, being pushed savagely by the rest of the reporters in the long line. "Mike! Get the camera rolling, dammit!" One of the lounging camera operators on the other side of Jojum's body straightened and shouldered his camera.

"This is Nick Steel, MKBM News Alive, coming to you from the Pyramid. I'm ashamed, deeply ashamed Good God, is this what the media has come to? Well, not us at MKBM News, not on your life, nor on his—this poor victim of my senseless, spiteful colleagues—colleagues, how that sad truth galls me—"

Max sighed. It was true, some things he was going to miss in the monastery, but, truth be told, television news wasn't one of them.

Miraculously flung half a block from the 57 Wells, Joey "Rip" Sanger and John Gully strode quietly down the street. Each had faced death, had seen with wide open eyes down its black, depthless maw, and each had emerged greatly changed, delivered, as it were, into a new, bright, promising world.

Joey well knew the Red Cap had survived, somewhere, and the mantle of the Sanger legend had fallen to the boy, and it didn't matter if he was ready for it or not, because that was the way of such things, to have it thrust upon you, leaving you no choice but to make do with what's landed in your lap. *He'll do fine. So will Chan—just one more accident report to file, at least it straightened his back even if his head, striking dead-on that lamp post, was pushed right in until his eyes barely looked over his collarbone. A survivable wound, for Wild Bill Chan. They'll do all right, they'll all do all right.*

"Whatcha planning now, Gully?"

The philosopher shrugged. "Leave the world-changing efforts to Art."

"Art?"

"Arthur Revell. You see him anywhere?"

"Uh, no, I don't."

"Exactly, he's been saved, twice, once by his own revelation, and once by someone else—whoever she might be. He's slipped back into the cracks, and you'll know in the years to come, as those cracks start spreading, that he's quietly doing his work, going about the task of intellectual disobedience, defying the rules of constraint, defying even the conventions of propriety, no matter what the context. As it all crumbles, my friend, you'll know where it started. Right here, right now."

"Hot damn," Joey sighed. "What a night. And you, Gully?"

"Not sure. I think I'm done, for a while at least. You?"

"Same for me."

They walked on in silence for a long time after that, and moments before they disappeared from view, their hands simultaneously linked—not in any sexual way of course, but in a manly, proper way—and then they were gone.

Leaving at long last the end of the octopod's tale. Kit and Moopsy found Andrew clawing his way out of the mangled back door of the Pyramid. After a long chase, Kit lassoed his former master in a wheat field and trussed the gibbering man up and then unceremoniously dragged him towards a hilltop (really just a rise, but for prairie folk it was a hill, damn near a mountain) where waited a flying saucer. Its ramp was down, and two other octopods riding dogs patrolled the perimeter.

Kit rode Moopsy up the ramp, dragging a weeping Andy Breech in their wake, and then inside, into the blinding white light where there waited an examination table, and odd-shaped instruments with which to probe Andrew's shrunken genitals for all eternity.

After a moment the outriders also entered the shimmering craft. The ramp rose flush with the saucer's underbelly. The vessel lifted into the nightsky and climbed blindingly fast into the heavens.

Annie Trollop had been crushed ignobly in the rush and subsequent tumble down the endless steps of the Pyramid. So badly mangled was she that no one knew her, no one at all. Brandon Safeword's body still haunts the alleys and streets of the city, seeking a head worthy of its astonishingly fit and trim body; and Penny Foote-Koobie lived her dreams out in the company of an increasingly exhausted but otherwise contented neanderthal, who eventually gave up painting and became a stock analyst for four years before returning to his roots and a reunion with nature and the Mother and the cycles of life and death that, generally speaking, are packed with a lot of death.

Arthur Revell and Faye disappeared, but don't be fooled. They're out there. *Doing art and thereby conspiring the ruination of modern civilization.*

Hah hah! Ho ho!